DATE DUE			4 / 01
AUG 16 '01			
NOV 19 '01			
JUN 21 '02			
GAYLORD			PRINTED IN U.S.A.

Survival
of the
Fittest

Edward Myers

Montemayor Press
Millburn, New Jersey

Printed in the United States of America.
For information contact
Montemayor Press,
P. O. Box 526, Millburn, NJ 07041
Web site: MontemayorPress.com

1 3 5 7 9 10 8 6 4 2

Library of Congress Cataloging-in-Publication Data

Myers, Edward. Survival of the Fittest/Edward
Myers—1st ed.
p. cm.

Summary: Rus, Jodie, and Matt survive the crash of a
small plane in the Peruvian rainforest and must endure
a multitude of physical and psychological hardships as
they attempt to reach safety.
ISBN 0-9674477-2-0 (trade)
[1. Brothers and sisters—Fiction. 2. Cousins—Fiction.
3. Survival—Fiction. 4. Rainforest—Fiction.
5. Peru—Fiction.] I. Title.
2000
[Fic]—00-090912 CIP AC

Printed in the United States by
Morris Publishing
3212 East Highway 30
Kearney, NE 68847
1-800-650-7888

For Cory—

Explorer of Worlds

Acknowledgments

I would never have written this book without the thoughtful, generous help of the management and staff of Amazonia Expeditions, especially Paul Beaver, Ph.D., Dolly Arévalo Beaver, Walter Soplín Culqui, Rudy Flores Lozano, and Juan Salas Ríos.

Most of all I'd like to thank my daughter, Robin, for her excellent company, observations, and insights during our travels in Peru; my wife, Edith Poor, for her support both before and during the writing phase; Sue Teasdale for her technical advice on aviation issues; Ann Tobias for her editorial guidance; and Julie Albright, Anita Diamant, Jane Folger, Delia Marshall, and Martha Santiuste for their many insights and suggestions regarding the book.

That which does not destroy me
will only make me stronger.

—Friederich Nietzsche

Part One

The Plane

1

TRUST

he wrote in the moisture condensing on the front window of the airport waiting lounge. But how? Trust people, Rus Cooper told himself, and they always let you down.

Jack's plane was already hours late. Now and then Rus looked up, staring through the glass at what lay beyond. The airport tarmac. Luggage carts piled with suitcases and boxes. Some parked airplanes: two old prop planes and a small new jet. The runway. A fence. And, just past the fence, great thickets of vegetation—palms, bushes, big leafy trees, tangled vines—interrupted here and there by thatched cottages. The rainforest.

Rus glanced at his watch. Why should he have felt surprised? People say they'll come, but they don't show up. They say they'll help, but they just go about their own business. They say they'll care, but they look after themselves instead. How long can you tolerate so much betrayal before it gets corrosive?

He rubbed out the initial T.

RUST

You really can't afford to rely on anyone. Not for anything. And where does that leave you?

He rubbed out the other T.

RUS

Here's where it leaves you, he thought: sitting in the airport near Iquitos, Peru, waiting and waiting for

1

Jack Cooper, who is Matt's and Jodie's father and who, having once been Rus's uncle, is now his father, too.

The airport was unlike any Rus had ever seen. Back in the States, you couldn't wait anywhere but in the waiting lounge. Here you could go almost anywhere without anyone giving a hoot. Growing restless, he opened the door and stepped outside, onto the tarmac. Then his cousins—his brother and sister, Rus reminded himself with a laugh—left the lounge, too, and followed him to the baggage area. They were now just a few dozen yards from the nearest aircraft. Rus could have walked right over to the parked planes, could have touched them, could have climbed aboard to explore them. Instead, he simply sat on his day pack and waited for Jack to arrive.

So far this trip had been everything he'd dreaded. Hours and hours on the plane from Newark to Miami. The luggage mix-up at the Miami airport. The long wait there. Then another flight, this time from Miami to Iquitos. Now the delay in Jack's arrival. Worst of all, the constant, inescapable presence of Matt and Jodie. The combined hassles were almost more than Rus could tolerate. There ought to be a law, he told himself, that someone his age, thirteen, shouldn't have to endure the company of younger kids longer than a few hours. Or maybe ten minutes.

"Dad's plane," Jodie announced. She stood a short distance to his left. Though dressed in shorts, a T-shirt, and sneakers, she looked so prim and proper that she might as well have been wearing one of those flowery dresses she wore on special occasions. What a princess, Rus thought. Probably afraid she'll muss her clothing if she sits on a suitcase. Gazing out at the runway, Jodie watched a small plane landing. Her dark brown ponytail swayed as she tracked the aircraft's progress from right to left.

"Maybe, maybe not," Rus said.

"It's him." She smiled, flashing her braces.

How could an eleven-year-old, he wondered, be so gullible?

"Here it comes!" Matt shouted.

Rus turned to see his other cousin about a dozen feet to the left. Matt was eight, dark-haired like his sister, and endlessly energetic. Worse yet, he was very smart, well aware of being smart, and eager to remind Rus and everyone else about his smartness. Matt had spent the last few hours building a complicated spaceship out of Legos; now he zoomed around, making rocket noises. He wasn't doing any harm, but all the racing back and forth had driven Rus half-crazy.

"Knock it off, would you?"

"You can't make me."

Rus tried another approach: "Strict orders from Mission Control."

"No way."

"Calling Professor Invento," Rus said. "Return to base, Professor Invento."

"Don't call me Professor Invento."

Rus decided to ignore him. Matt considered himself the world's greatest eight-year-old inventor. Right now he claimed to be testing the first fusion-powered transport. He was so caught up in his fantasy that he'd almost gotten hit by a motorized baggage cart. Would he survive long enough to see his dad's plane arrive? Maybe, maybe not. Rus didn't really care.

A goofy-looking plane taxied toward the airport terminal. Much smaller than a jet airliner but bigger than a private plane, it had high wings, two propeller engines, and five or six windows on each side. Words on the fuselage read UNITED MEDICAL MISSIONS. So Jodie was right after all. Luckily, she spared Rus one of her I-told-you-so glances; she only cupped her hands against her ears while Matt hollered incomprehensibly over the aircraft noise. Pathetic! Yet Rus felt no excitement at the thought of Jack's arrival—just a dull sense of relief. At least someone else could deal with these two brats for a while.

3

Only one person emerged from the plane, and it wasn't Jack. Short and wide, with black hair and a black mustache, he wore a rumpled pilot's uniform and a slightly flattened pilot's cap that looked as if he'd sat on it. He crossed the tarmac toward the baggage area. "You are Jack's children?" he asked in accented English.

Matt asked, "Where's Dad?"

The man gestured with a folded piece of paper. "Your father, he could not leave the clinic. An emergency."

"Is he okay?" Jodie asked, looking alarmed.

"He is fine. Just very—" The pilot switched to Spanish: *"Muy ocupado."*

"Busy?"

"He sends you this message."

Rus took the paper.

> *Sat.–11:30 a.m.*
>
> Kids,
>
> We've got big problems here—
> I'm struggling to help the docs with a
> rush of surgeries. You'll be fine
> with Capt. Lozano, who's the pilot
> for the clinic. He'll bring you to
> Nuevo Belén. See you this evening!
>
> Love to all—
>
> Dad

"He's not coming?" Jodie asked in bewilderment.

"Surprise," Rus said.

Captain Lozano smiled and gestured toward the plane. "We should go."

4

Jodie looked uneasy. "Are you sure this is what Dad wants?" she asked.

"He waits for you," said the captain.

Rus shrugged. "That's his handwriting. It's the clinic's plane. Let's just get it over with."

Matt started jumping up and down. "It's a Badger!" he shouted gleefully. "A turboprop!"

Rus stared at the plane and then reluctantly followed the pilot as he led Jodie and Matt across the tarmac. He wasn't eager to be cooped up with his cousins yet again, but even another flight in their company seemed better than staying in Iquitos. As for what was still ahead: he wouldn't count on anything—or anyone. He'd wait and see. He'd follow his hunches. He'd look after himself.

Waiting to take his turn to climb the little folding staircase into the plane, Rus used a finger to write in the condensation on the fuselage:

TRUST

RUST

RUS

2

Jodie was frustrated that her father hadn't come out to meet them. The plan had been that she and Matt and Rus would find him waiting in Iquitos. They'd all fly to Nuevo Belén. They'd spend a week with Dad at the rainforest clinic where he spent two months each year as a surgical technician. When Dad finished his volunteer work, the Coopers would travel home together, from Nuevo Belén to Iquitos to Miami to New Jersey. All the arrangements had been made in advance. So why had Dad changed plans so abruptly?

Boarding the plane, Jodie realized that the flight itself wasn't what troubled her. Relying on unfamiliar people wasn't a problem, either. She didn't even worry about traveling hundreds of miles into the rainforest. But surviving another few hours of Matt and Rus's company? Now *that* was a challenge.

"Wow, what a weird configuration!" Matt exclaimed, settling into his seat.

At first Jodie didn't know what he meant by "configuration," but she soon understood. The plane's interior didn't resemble any she'd seen before. There was the cockpit up front, of course, and that looked pretty typical: two seats, some small windows, a zillion dials and switches. The cabin, though, was just a big open space. The only seats were at the rear—four of them—and they faced backwards.

"But I guess it makes sense," Matt went on. "They use this plane mostly to transport medical supplies and stuff. So of *course* they've configured it—"

"Spare me," Rus groaned.

"—for cargo."

They took their seats. Jodie sat with Matt on one side of the aisle; Rus sat alone on the other. Jodie buckled her seat belt. She tried to ignore Matt's and Rus's bickering. Soon they fell silent. What a relief—at least until the silence, too, felt burdensome.

What bothered her wasn't just the nearly endless squabbles; it was knowing that things hadn't always been this way. Jodie and Matt had always been closer than most brothers and sisters. At times they had looked so much alike—dark-haired, brown-eyed, and fairly short— that they sometimes pretended they were twins. They had their ups and downs, and sometimes they argued. But mostly they got along. They didn't hassle each other when their interests differed, and they enjoyed doing things together—swimming, hiking, making art projects. Nobody made a big deal of their friendship; it was simply there, and good.

Then Rus arrived and everything changed. Of course, Jodie had known him since she was a baby. They played together a few times a year when Aunt Alice, Dad's only sister, traveled from Iowa to visit the Coopers in New Jersey. Jodie had always dreaded those visits. Rus behaved worse than even the brattiest kids at school. He teased his cousins. He picked fights. He stole Jodie's watch and blamed it on Matt. He took the aquarium's lid off and let Snooker, Jodie's cat, "go fishing." Luckily the visits were short, so Jodie tried hard to stay patient. As Mom and Dad told her, "Rus needs your kindness." He was an only child. He didn't have a dad. His mom was an alcoholic, she couldn't keep a job, and she had lots of money problems. So just as Mom and Dad tried to help Alice, Jodie tried to help Rus. Maybe putting up with him for a few days each year wasn't asking much.

Then Alice got sick and couldn't take care of Rus. Mom and Dad offered to look after him. Rus moved in— not for keeps, as Jodie's parents told her, but only till Alice recovered. But Alice didn't recover. She got worse and worse, then died. What had started out as a long visit *was* for keeps. And somehow everything had changed.

Something caught her attention: the engines firing up. They started with a whine. Then each propeller began to blur, and the noise increased to a roar.

"This is *so cool!*" Matt hollered, bouncing in his seat, the safety belt scarcely able to restrain him. At least his interest in the engines kept him in place: he gazed out the window as if at the world's most fascinating TV show.

Seated beside him, Jodie couldn't see much; Matt's head blocked her view. She sat back in her seat and stared at the rear of the aircraft.

Suddenly it occurred to her what she didn't like about this arrangement: flying backwards. Even riding backwards in a station wagon made her feel queasy. How could she tolerate going so much faster in a plane?

Soon the plane taxied down the runway.

The rainforest, Jodie reassured herself. For years she'd wanted to see the rainforest. She wasn't pleased to have Rus along, and she would have preferred to be rid of him altogether, but if his presence was part of the deal—well, she'd tolerate him.

As the plane rose and the land spread out below her, Jodie realized that she'd finally have what she wanted. She would walk beneath a canopy whose leaves sifted sunlight onto the forest floor below. She would canoe down rivers as peaceful as the surrounding silence. She would cast her baited hook into waters so full of fish that catching dinner would be almost effortless. She would marvel at a hundred species of birds—hawks, owls, toucans, larks, parrots, kingfishers—while they pranced among the branches. She would spot monkeys swinging from limb to limb. She would coax humming-birds into alighting on her open palms. She would even help out at the clinic. She would live with the villagers, find friends among the children, earn respect and admiration for her good-heartedness and sense of humor, then return home with a hundred stories about her adventures in this tropical paradise.

3

The Badger was the coolest plane Matt had ever seen. It was much smaller than a jet airliner but looked big inside because it was almost empty—it felt like sitting in a big metal can! It had huge oval windows, too, so Matt could look out and see the whole left wing, the engine mounted there, and the gray disc of the spinning propeller. He loved the noise: a great buzzy scream. Sitting in such a loud plane made Matt feel powerful. And because the plane flew much lower than a jet, he could see the clouds and the rivers and even the rough textures of the jungle.

"Isn't this cool!" he told his sister.

He couldn't hear Jodie's voice but saw her mouth say *What?*

"This is cool!"

"What!"

He waved her away. "Never mind!" Waste of time, he told himself. Jodie never understood the beauty of planes, trains, cars, trucks, backhoes, bulldozers, or any other machine. All she really cared about was *nature.* Even now Matt could see her gazing out at the clouds and jungle below the clouds popcorn scattered on a dark green carpet—when she could have been enjoying the plane itself. *Girls! Give them a great ride like this and they don't even appreciate it!* But at least Jodie wasn't as bad as Rus, who didn't appreciate anything at all.

Thinking of Rus made Matt turn to his left. There he was, right across the aisle: the world's worst grouch. Matt couldn't see his face—Rus had turned away to stare out the window—but Matt didn't need to see him. He knew what he'd look like. Tall. Big-shouldered. Much lighter than Jodie or Matt: pale, blond, blue-eyed. Serious, too. Always serious. What was Jodie's word for him? *Somber!* Sort of sleepy-looking, only sad at the same time.

Which made sense in some ways. The guy had been through a lot. His mom had always drunk too much, she got sick, and she died. But why, Matt wondered, did Rus have to be so darn *grumpy* about it? Like nobody else had any problems! Matt had broken his arm once, and last year a bully named Theo had socked him in the nose. And it wasn't as if nothing good had ever happened to Rus. Matt's family had taken him in. They'd actually adopted him! Was that so terrible? Matt had even offered to share his bedroom with Rus, who said "Sure," moved right in, took over like he owned the place, and never once said thank you. Now Rus even got to visit Peru—the trip Mom and Dad had always promised Matt and Jodie—and acted like it was *his* trip, with everyone else just coming along for the ride.

Matt felt glad the plane was so noisy: he could ignore his cousin.

They flew for a long time. Matt wasn't sure how long. Outside the plane, the rainforest stretched out forever. Bumpy green trees. Snaky rivers, mostly brown. Now and then little glinty patches by the water—maybe villages? He wondered how long they'd fly. An hour? Longer? He couldn't even guess. It was late afternoon already.

Matt started to feel hungry. That was the only thing about this plane he didn't like: there was no flight attendant to offer him a snack. The more he thought about his hunger, the hungrier he felt.

Matt unbuckled his seat belt, got up, and started to move around. It wasn't easy—he didn't have an aisle to walk down, bracing himself against the upright seat backs. The cabin sank, rose, sank again. Matt lost his balance several times, crouched to avoid a fall, and even crawled on all fours at one point. He reached the cockpit, though, without getting hurt. The door was open. "Excuse me?"

No answer. The pilots sat there flying the plane. "Hey!"

10

The captain turned suddenly. Smiling, he asked, "Is there a problem?"

"I'm sorta hungry." Captain Lozano just stared at him, so Matt made an eating motion with his right hand.

"Oh, sorry," said the captain. "We brought nothing—such a short flight."

Retreating, Matt went back to the cabin. He had bought some candy in the Miami airport but planned to save it for the stay with Dad. Wasn't there anything else to eat on board? Staggering toward his seat, he sized up the cabin. Five or six big plastic jugs filled with water. Some boxes marked UNITED MEDICAL MISSIONS. A roll of clear plastic like the kind painters use to protect floors from spattering paint. Not much else. The kids' suitcases were locked up in the cargo hold, and the only luggage inside the cabin was their day packs.

Matt decided to raid his stash of candy. He lurched toward his pack.

Just then he heard an odd noise: a change in the engine's hum that sounded like a lawnmower hitting a patch of weeds.

The plane jolted once, twice, three times. Matt worried about losing his balance, so he decided to forget about the candy; instead, he worked his way back to his seat and fastened his seatbelt.

"What's going on?" Jodie asked.

"Turboprops are real loud," Matt told her. "You have noise from—"

"Shut up a second!"

Matt tried to figure out what his sister had noticed.

The plane started to sink. He glanced over at Rus, who glanced back, then turned away. He looked at Jodie.

"Something's wrong," she said.

Matt felt shocked by how pale she looked.

The plane jolted hard, then tilted to the right.

Matt looked out the window and saw to his amazement that the left propeller had stopped. The plane seemed much quieter now.

Then a new noise reached him: the pilots hollering at each other. Matt couldn't understand them, since they spoke in Spanish, but he could tell they were upset. The fear in their voices worried him.

Suddenly the copilot rushed over and leaned across Jodie to stare through the window at the engine. He shouted in Spanish so loud that he spattered Matt with saliva. Then he staggered away and headed for the cockpit. The two men started hollering again.

A strange tingle ran through Matt's body. It reminded him of last winter, when he had unscrewed a Christmas tree light bulb and poked a finger into the socket. His whole body had felt like it was melting, and all he could say was *"Uhhhhhhhh!"* He felt like that now, only without the socket and the electricity.

"Jodie!" Matt screeched. "What's happening?"

"I don't know!"

Staring at Jodie, Matt wanted to grab her hand but didn't: Rus might call him a sissy.

Then the other engine—the one near Rus's side of the plane—started to struggle. Matt heard a strange whine and a sputtering noise. Soon that engine, too, fell silent.

Matt couldn't believe it. Now *both* engines had stopped! Instead of their loud, lulling roar Matt now heard only a spooky whistle.

"Rus—"

No response.

"Rus!"

His cousin turned toward him briefly, then away. It almost seemed as if Rus didn't see him. Then Rus bolted from his seat and stumbled over to the cockpit. "What's going on!" he shouted at the pilots. Matt couldn't tell if the men were shouting at Rus or at each other. Rus called out again: "So *do* something!"

The plane tilted steeply, nose downward. Matt expected more noise—a shriek, a rumble, an explosion—but he heard only that same weird whistle.

He didn't know what to do. Matt wanted someone to tell him everything would be okay. He wanted someone to say that the plane wouldn't crash. The plane's

12

silence terrified him. *Would* it crash? *This isn't happening,* Matt told himself.

He heard shouting from the cockpit. Rus. The pilot. The co-pilot. A scratchy voice on the radio.

Rus suddenly came back, cursing, and strapped himself into his seat.

The plane tilted to the left. When he looked out the window, Matt could see the land more clearly now. What had been misty gray-green below looked darker and rougher. Sunlight flashed on a river. He spotted some specks that might have been houses. Everything rushed away.

Jodie was shaking hard, but Matt couldn't tell if she shook from fear or from the plane's motions, which rattled him till his teeth chattered.

"Jodie—"

"What!"

"Are we—?" Matt couldn't even finish the sentence. He needed someone to hold him. He grabbed at the armrest between them, found Jodie's right hand there, and clutched it. Wouldn't she protect him? She had always protected him in the past. Jodie, his big sister, wouldn't let anything bad happen to him.

"Do *this,*" Jodie said just then. She slumped forward, pressing her chest against her thighs and hiding her face against her folded arms the way the safety information cards on the big jet airliners had showed them.

The Badger jolted twice, hard. Matt wondered, *Is this the crash?* But the plane just kept sinking. Matt felt so scared he thought he might pee his pants. Anything but *that,* he told himself—Rus would never let him forget it!

Not knowing what else to do, Matt leaned forward, too, like Jodie. Then, despite his fear, something occurred to him that made him sit upright. "Wait!" he shouted. "That position is if you're facing *forward!*"

Jodie looked confused. "What?"

Matt told her, "We're facing *backward.*"

"Right, but how does that—"

13

"So sit up straight," Matt yelled. "Won't these backward seats protect us?"

They both sat back, shoving their bodies against the seats. Matt held Jodie's hand so hard that his fingers hurt. *Please don't crash!* he shouted in the silence of his mind. *Please don't crash!*

More jolts. The whole plane shivered.

Matt looked over at Rus. He called out to him: once, twice, three times. The plane was so quiet that he must have heard, but Rus didn't respond. He sat upright, too, just like Jodie and Matt, but only gazed straight ahead.

"Rus—"

Matt remembered a wisecrack he'd made about his cousin's name a long time ago: *Your mom is so poor, she can't even afford the extra S to spell your name right!*

As if Rus had heard Matt's thoughts, he turned just then to face him. He glanced at Matt. And, despite the sight of the trees now skimming right below—so close that Matt could imagine reaching down and touching the leaves like a kid in a canoe dipping his fingers into the water—Rus turned away once more and scrunched his eyes shut.

Suddenly Matt saw water out there, real water, brown water, just a few feet below. The Badger sank toward it. And at once the plane started rattling, rattled hard, stopped rattling as it rose briefly, then sank again, hit the water, and rattled so violently that it must surely have been falling apart. There was a weird metallic groaning noise. Matt felt his body shake till his bones hurt.

The rattling grew and grew until Matt heard the loudest noise in the world.

And then the loudest silence.

14

Part Two

The River

4

Are you. . . fine?

Are you. . . fine?

Rus struggled for a long time to decide who was speaking. It couldn't have been Mom. Aunt Penny? No, this voice sounded too high for Penny. One of his foster parents, then? Maybe it was Mrs. Jasper, who sounded like Mickey Mouse. Or Mr. Nolan, whose voice was higher than his wife's.

Are you. . . fine?

Only one problem: those people didn't really care if Rus was fine! And why would anyone put the question like that instead of asking, "Are you all right?"

Are you. . . fine?

No, Rus told himself, he wasn't fine. He wasn't fine at all. His whole body ached, and his neck, especially, hurt like crazy.

Are you. . . fine?

He thought, *No way I'm fine!*

Then, realizing that it wasn't a human voice he heard, Rus opened his eyes.

The plane. The rainforest.

There was no motion, no sound except for a ticking noise and, in the distance, a three-note cry that rose at the end like a question: *Are you. . . fine?* Then, closer, a different sound: a moan.

He looked to his right and saw who made it. Jodie. Or maybe Matt. They sat slumped together in their seats.

Rus turned the other way and looked out the window. All he could see was something green shoved against the glass.

Matt began to cry.

"Where's Dad?" Jodie asked, looking around.

"I don't know!" Rus hollered abruptly. "Let's just get out before this plane starts to burn!"

They didn't move. Jodie and Matt only whined and clung to each other. What was that ticking noise? He noticed a bad smell, too, something sharp and electrical.

"Let's get out of here!"

His cousins kept whimpering.

"See you later," Rus announced. He forced himself up, stumbled into the plane's cargo area, shoved open the door, stepped through the doorway, and forced his way through a tangle of vegetation so dense that it grabbed at him like a net.

"Are you all right?" Jodie asked, shaking her brother. "Matt! Matt, answer me!"

He wasn't unconscious yet he didn't respond. With his knees pulled up to his chest and his arms wrapped around his head, he wouldn't stop trembling.

"Matt—stop it!"

She didn't know what to do. Her hands and legs shook and a swell of nausea rose from her belly till she almost vomited. Somehow she kept hold of herself. *The plane has crashed,* Jodie told herself, *but we're still alive.* She wanted to leave this place more than anything, but she couldn't imagine abandoning Matt, so she took hold of his arm and started tugging.

"Leave me alone!" he yelled.

"Come on, darn it!"

"Just leave me alone!"

No matter how hard she pulled, she couldn't budge him. Matt was only eight but incredibly strong. How would she get him out of there? Then she thought of the pilots. She'd get Captain Lozano's help and they'd carry him off the plane.

Jodie swung around, stumbled over some stuff on the floor, and reached out to brace herself against the bulkhead at the rear of the cockpit.

18

But the bulkhead wasn't there. *Trees* were there. A big reddish-brown trunk on the left, a smaller trunk and some green branches on the right. Metal, too: twisted, bent, smashed. Tangles of wire. Some fractured plastic panels. All this stuff was now jumbled together so tightly that Jodie couldn't remember how the plane had ever been something in which people could *fit*.

She backed off at once and returned to her brother. "Matt—"

"I don't like this!" he wailed, his eyes pinched shut. "I don't like this!"

She realized only then that she'd have to use her secret weapon. She'd do what she always did when everything else had failed to get Matt moving.

"Kootchie-kootchie!" she said, and she began to tickle him.

"Stop!"

"Kootchie-koo!"

"Stop it!"

Jodie tickled him till he laughed, till he batted at her hands, till he forced himself up and, trying to avoid her, stumbled toward the doorway and off the plane.

He'd run away, escape the forest, leave Peru, and never come back. He'd flee from these people—the pilot, the copilot, Jodie, Rus—and leave them far behind. Matt was a fast runner and no one could catch him. They couldn't make him do what he didn't want to. He didn't want to be there. All he wanted was to go home and be with Mom and Dad where he was safe, so he ran and ran.

Something snagged his ankles, tripped him, and sent him flying. He hit the ground face-first. His head, hands, chest, and knees hurt so much that Matt couldn't breathe right, and for a moment he almost passed out.

Someone said, "It's all right, it's all right," and he couldn't struggle any more. He just held handfuls of something and pressed his forehead to the ground.

19

"Matt, we're okay"—that was Jodie's voice.

"The plane crashed," he told her.

"I know that."

"I'm scared!" He kept remembering the silence as the plane descended.

"I'm scared, too," she said, "but we're okay. Just shook up."

He forced his eyes open. Leaves lay all around, and his hands clutched still more leaves. Jodie crouched nearby. Her presence at his side reassured him. But she was a kid—his sister. Who was in charge? "Where's Rus?" he asked.

"Around here someplace."

"Where's the pilots?" Surely Captain Lozano would help them.

"I think they got squished."

"Squished!"

"Well, *just look,*" Jodie said, pushing his face with her hands and making him gaze at the wreckage. "The front is all shoved in—"

"Jodie—"

"—and the pilots are still in there."

"Jodie—" Matt felt a sinking sensation deep inside his belly. It scared him to think of the captain and the copilot trapped inside the Badger's smashed front end. The only grown-ups present had died. His vision grew blurry. His throat tightened. In a voice so squeaky that he almost couldn't talk, Matt asked, "What are we going to do?"

"I don't know," Jodie answered softly.

Matt didn't, either. And so, scared and sore, he did the only thing that made sense after surviving a plane crash in the rainforest: he lay down and began to cry.

5

The plane didn't burn. It just sat there, bent and bashed and torn, so densely surrounded by trees and bushes that it might have been lying in the jungle fifteen years instead of fifteen minutes. No sizzle of sparks. No crackle of flames. No great billowing explosion, like in the movies. Just the plane and the jungle and Rus, a dozen yards off, staring at the plane and the jungle.

It was hard to be sure, but Rus thought he understood what had happened. When the engines quit, the pilots had managed to guide the plane down. Down *where*, though? The rainforest was flat, but the endless expanse of trees must have made it nearly impossible to find a good landing place. Obviously Captain Lozano had failed to find one. What options had that left? Crashing straight into the jungle—or else locating the only thing here that resembled a runway: a straight stretch of river. He'd scarcely pulled it off. He'd found a good place and brought the plane down on the water, but he'd run out of room. The plane must have been moving fast when the river curved to the left; the Badger jumped the bank and plowed into the trees. So here they were.

Surprise, surprise, Rus thought. So far everything else had gone wrong; why shouldn't the plane crash, too? That was certainly the most spectacular way for people to let him down. What could top a plane crash?

Nothing happened. Nothing at all. If anything, this place was eerily calm. Rus heard lots of bird song—chirps, hoots, shrieks, and that distant three-note cry—but otherwise the jungle couldn't have been much more peaceful. No voices. No rumble of cars and trucks. No racket from other machines. No radios, TVs, or sirens. When a bug buzzed by, the noise startled him.

21

Then another sound caught his attention: weeping. He looked around, saw at once that it came from Matt and Jodie a short distance ahead, and he turned away from them at once. Typical. Let them bawl their eyes out. The Princess and Professor Invento! It was their eagerness to visit Peru that had gotten him stuck here anyway.

Something hit him just then, a pain he dreaded feeling, a deep sense of longing for his mother. At once he shoved that emotion away.

Yet he felt almost the same way he'd felt on learning of Mom's death: scared about what would happen next; angry that people had left him in the lurch again; confused, weary, and alone.

But he also felt *intent*. Intent on taking care of himself. Intent on himself.

In some ways, he decided, everything had changed; in other ways, nothing. He was still Rus Cooper. He still knew he was smart enough to do whatever needed to be done. Even before his mother died, Rus had relied on his own wits to survive. He'd looked after Mom more than she'd ever looked after him. He'd managed to keep up appearances for the neighbors and his teachers when Mom went on her drinking binges. He'd outfoxed the Iowa City social workers into thinking things were fine when they weren't. When Mom's situation worsened and Rus got placed with those foster families, he had made sure no one took advantage of him. If he wanted to stay, he stayed; if he wanted to leave, he left. The same was true when Mom got sick and his aunt and uncle had taken him in. Rus ran his own show, he told himself. No one told Rus Cooper what to do.

He'd manage. He'd do whatever he needed to.

Even in the middle of the rainforest.

Though dizzy and sore, Jodie felt more concerned about Matt than about herself. She couldn't make him stop crying. He huddled on the ground and sobbed.

22

Trying hard to cheer him up, Jodie said the first thing that occurred to her: "Isn't this like the beginning of *The Wizard of Oz*? The house comes crashing down. Dorothy opens the door and steps out. And suddenly the whole world is different—beautiful and lush!"

These words succeeded in stopping Matt's tears, but not in the way Jodie had expected. He sat up, wiped his face, and stared at her. "What did you say?"

She tried to gesture casually. "*The Wizard of*, you know, *Oz*."

"That's the stupidest thing I've ever heard."

"It was a joke."

"Jodie, our plane crashes and you think it's like *The Wizard of Oz!*"

"All I mean is, things are different now. Completely different." She couldn't believe he'd taken her so seriously. In the past they didn't argue; they'd tease and kid each other, but it was never serious. Once Rus had joined the family, though. . .

Oddly, it was Rus who now stepped in to prevent an argument. "Stop hassling each other," he told them. "We're in a real mess—"

"Okay, okay."

"—and we'd better do something about it."

"All right!" Jodie shouted. "What should we do?"

Rus glanced at his watch. "You know what time it is? After six. It'll be dark soon. Doesn't that bother you?"

"I guess so," Matt said, shrugging.

"You *guess* so."

That did it. Exasperated, Jodie walked away from her brother and her cousin. She took a few steps toward the wrecked airplane. Feeling spooked by the sight, though, she veered to the left. She simply walked down the path the Badger had cut through the forest before it came to rest.

She didn't know what to think. This situation *was* like *The Wizard of Oz*, Jodie told herself. Just like Dorothy Gale, Jodie had fallen from the sky. Now everything was different. Beautiful and lush? Yes, she noted, easing past some squat little palm trees and stepping over a cluster of fan-like ferns. Beautiful and lush.

The ground sloped. Following it gently downward, she found herself abruptly standing beside a river.

Reaching water wasn't what surprised her; Jodie knew that they'd survived only because Captain Lozano had found a river big enough to allow an emergency landing. But she hadn't thought a river in Peru could be so—*little*. This was the rainforest! The Amazon basin! Weren't the rivers here all mighty torrents?

What Jodie saw couldn't have been more than sixty feet across. The water, which looked smooth and light-brown, like the *café au lait* her mother drank each morning, moved so slowly that Jodie detected its motion only by watching some bubbles on its surface. It made no noise. Not a rumble, not a gurgle, not a splash, not a hiss. Great puddles of light shimmered on the water. The shadows of trees massed at the edges. At another time, she would have found this scene wonderfully calm and peaceful; now it chilled her. What was this place? Where had they ended up? Gazing at this river, she suddenly shivered from the deepest, sharpest fear she had ever felt.

Matt listened to Rus and Jodie argue for a long time. His head pounded, his stomach cramped, and his neck and back hurt. He couldn't really concentrate, but this big argument kept grabbing his attention. Jodie and Rus couldn't agree on anything, and they got more and more annoyed at each other as they argued. For a while Matt worried that they might even start hitting—they stood close and yelled face-to-face—but then they backed off, paced around, and argued at a distance.

24

"So let's radio for help," Jodie suggested. "You know—using the plane's radio."

"Great idea!" Rus said, clapping his hands just once. "If you can somehow squeeze into the cockpit, find the radio, pry it out, and get it to work, then be my guest."

Matt got up, walked over to the plane, and stared at it for a long time. He couldn't believe he'd survived. It sickened him to think that the pilots hadn't. The thought of their bodies inside the wreck gave him the creeps.

"So what are we supposed to do?" Jodie asked Rus.

"How should *I* know?" Rus muttered. "I don't know the first thing about this stinking place. You're the little nature girl."

Fed up, Matt walked away from his sister and his cousin. Let them argue. He felt too hungry to care. If only he could have a snack. . . He felt uneasy entering the plane again, but he stepped on board anyway and looked around.

The plane was almost empty. Once again he saw the big plastic water jugs, the boxes marked UNITED MEDICAL MISSIONS, and the wide roll of plastic, but that was all. Just their luck: they'd crash-landed with so few supplies. And no food.

Then he spotted his backpack. The candy! At once he raced over to the pack, grabbed it, and leaped outside again. "Hey!" Matt yelled. "Look at this!"

"What is it?" Jodie asked, rushing over.

"My pack!" He shook the pack once and all his candy fell out. "Ta da!"

Two or three Snickers. . . Two Milky Ways. . . Two bags of M&Ms. . . A pack of Twizzlers. . . A couple of Kit-Kats. . . There must have been eight or ten packets.

"Whoa!" Jodie exclaimed. "Just like Halloween!"

Rus snatched up some candy bars and stuffed them in his pockets.

Matt was outraged. "What are you doing!"

25

"Just taking my share."

"Your *share?*"

"There's three of us, right, so a third of this stuff is mine."

Furious, Matt couldn't stop shaking. "Yeah, but—"

"What's the problem?" Rus demanded.

"We're gonna do this even-steven," Jodie announced, "so don't get grabby."

Rus slid both hands into his front pockets to lock their contents into place.

Matt looked at his stash of candy. He couldn't remember exactly how much he'd brought, but what lay on the ground looked like maybe half of it. How much had Rus taken? He'd moved so fast, Matt couldn't really tell. Four, maybe five candy bars.

Now Rus wandered off, stood a few paces away, and took out some candy. With his back to Matt and Jodie, he started eating it.

Jodie picked up a Milky Way and held it up to Matt. "Mind if I have this?"

"Be my guest," Matt said.

She peeled the wrapper and took a bite. At once she grinned. "Wow! That's the best!" She tilted her head back and laughed so hard that her ponytail jiggled.

Tempted by the sight of both Rus and Jodie eating, Matt picked up a Snickers, ripped open the wrapper, and started gobbling the candy. He couldn't imagine anything more delicious. Just a few bites finished it off.

Jodie guffawed. "I'm still hungry!"

"So am I."

The M&Ms and the Twizzlers lay on the ground before them. At once Matt picked up the candy, gave the Twizzlers to Jodie, and wolfed down the M&Ms.

"What d'you think Mom and Dad would say," Matt asked, his mouth full of chocolate, "if they knew our dinner was nothing but candy?"

"What you guys really ought to wonder about," Rus said suddenly, walking back, "is what you'll eat next time you're hungry."

Puzzled, Matt looked up at his cousin. "You mean tomorrow?"

Rus kicked some dead leaves. "Yeah, tomorrow. And the day after. And the day after that."

"Well, there's the other candy bars," Matt said.

"Which candy bars?" Rus asked.

"*You* know." Matt slapped his pants pockets and gestured at Rus.

"The only ones left are *my* share," Rus said. "You guys ate *your* share."

"But that's not fair—"

"You know what?" Jodie asked suddenly. "None of this really matters. 'Cause we don't have to worry about tomorrow or the day after tomorrow."

"No?" said Rus. "How come?"

"'Cause someone'll rescue us."

"You're sure about that?"

"You bet I'm sure," she said. "Remember when the plane was going down? Captain Lozano radioed for help. I heard him. All that shouting."

"Well, that's real reassuring," Rus said. "I'm always pleased to hear your sunny viewpoint. But of course you had a sunny view of this whole trip and look where we've ended up."

Matt watched Rus and Jodie as they argued. He wanted Jodie to win, yet he worried that this time she wasn't right. Rus's words scared him.

"Say whatever you like," Jodie told Rus. "I know we'll be okay. As soon as Dad reports us missing, lots of people will start looking for us."

"Yeah!" Matt shouted, trying to tip the balance in Jodie's favor.

"Fine," Rus said. "I didn't say they wouldn't look."

"So?"

He stretched, running his hands through his short blond hair. "Looking isn't the problem. They'll look and look. The problem is—will they *find* us?"

6

Night fell. Rus couldn't believe how quickly darkness came: flooding in like water. What had been a strange-looking place soon became a strange place he couldn't even see.

"I don't like this!" Matt whined as the last light faded.

"Neither do I," Rus told him, "but it'll be dark till dawn, right? Isn't that how it usually works? Better get used to it."

Jodie, a dim shape somewhere to his left, asked: "What are we going to *do*?"

Rus lost his temper. "Look, you guys do whatever you like, but I'm calling it a day. If you need me, I'll be snoozing in the plane." He took a few steps toward the dark outline of the wreckage.

"The *plane?*" Jodie blurted.

The fear Rus detected in those two words caught him short. "It's waterproof," he said. "It's away from the bugs. I can curl up on the seats."

"But there's *bodies* in there!" Matt exclaimed.

"Oh, come on."

"There's *no* way I'm going in sleep inside the plane," Jodie stated.

"Fine." Rus walked over to the wreckage. Stepping up into the big shadow that was the doorway, he entered the cargo area. He couldn't believe that Jodie and Matt were so superstitious that they'd pass up a relatively comfortable night just because of two corpses nearby.

He could barely see. Groping his way back to the seats, Rus tripped two or three times and barely kept his balance. He touched the bulkhead that separated the cargo area from the passenger area, located one of the arm rests, and eased his way into a seat. It would be great to be alone.

Two corpses. . . Suddenly terrified, Rus got up, stumbled forth, and leaped out through the doorway.

They ended up using the plane's tail as a shelter. It wasn't any worse than sleeping under a picnic table, Rus told himself, and he'd done *that* before. If nothing else, the tail might protect him if it rained.

But Matt started griping again: "I don't *like* this."

"You don't have to like it," Rus said. "Just put up with it."

"There's bugs here," Jodie complained.

She was right—bugs swarmed all around. Squads of mosquitoes whined all around, zeroing in like tiny fighter planes. Ants attacked from every direction. But so what? Rus couldn't do a thing about the bugs, so why bother? "Go to sleep," he told his cousins.

"Yeah, but how?"

"That's not my problem."

Yet no matter how hard he tried, Rus couldn't doze off, either. His back and neck hurt. His skin itched from dozens of bug bites. New bugs kept biting him. Strange sounds put him on edge: humming, buzzing, rustling noises; sudden laugh-like cries; hoots and shrieks. Just birds, he told himself. Or something. But the racket bothered him anyway. And at first he felt too hot, then gradually too cool. Rus couldn't recall having ever felt so tired, yet he simply couldn't fall asleep.

What bothered him most of all was his own thoughts. How could he have ended up in such a mess? As if things hadn't been bad enough already, now this! Not only was he stuck in the jungle—he was stuck with Matt and Jodie. Professor Invento and the Princess. The two most annoying kids on earth. Even now Rus could hear them whispering and whimpering just a few feet away. He couldn't imagine how he'd get out of this jam with Jodie and Matt dragging him down.

Maybe he wouldn't, Rus thought suddenly. Not if they clung to him. Which meant, Get rid of them. Kick free. Sink or swim.

Rus sat up. It wouldn't take much to sneak away. Were they sleeping? Hard to tell. What did it matter? A few steps and he'd be gone.

He'd done it before: he'd sneaked away from the Zelinskis' house one night; he'd bailed out of the Nolans' camping trip at an Iowa state park; he'd left other foster families behind. Compared to those escape jobs, this one would be a snap.

He stood carefully. One step. Two.

No one called out as he walked off. The only noise was the drone of bugs.

Sorry guys, Rus said silently. *It's the survival of the fittest.*

He felt thrilled to be alone. No more whiny cousins! Rus could clear out and leave this steamy jungle far behind. He'd hike to safety. Of course he wouldn't really abandon Matt and Jodie; his solo trek would actually speed their rescue. Rus would tell the authorities where to find the wrecked plane and the kids huddled near it. Simple as that. No doubt Jodie and Matt would bellyache later about Rus's departure. *He left us there!* they'd wail. *All by ourselves!* To which Rus would reply: *Get real. If I'd stayed there with you, we'd still be waiting by the wreckage. The only reason you're alive is I had the guts to clear out and do something.*

Rus moved slowly, proceeding by touch alone. Something rough and wide: a tree. A wobbly pole-like thing to the right: some sort of vine? Next to that, some tattered leaves: part of a palm tree? Rus couldn't move fast, but that didn't matter. Slow but sure. He'd ease away in the darkness. Then, once dawn arrived, he'd make faster progress.

31

Suddenly a noise startled him: a squeal so loud that Rus jolted back. A thrashing sound followed. Closer, closer, closer. . . Then something shoved hard against his legs and raced off to the right.

Panicking, Rus sprinted forward without knowing where to go. At once he bashed into something, whacked his forehead, staggered, and fell.

He lay there panting. What had he startled? A jaguar? A wild pig? Rus couldn't remember which animals lived in the jungle. His mind raced with terrifying thoughts. Was it gone now? He tried to calm himself but couldn't help but imagine wild beasts lurking, waiting to pounce, in the bushes.

When he backtracked, though, he wasn't sure which way to go. Only a few stars showed through the leaves overhead—too little light to show him a path. Rus groped around, touching leaves, vines, and bark, but he couldn't make sense of what he felt. This way or that? Ahead or back? He felt more and more frightened.

He reached out and pulled away when thorns raked his left forearm.

Gasping, trying not to curse, Rus suddenly wished he'd never left. He turned, reached out carefully, found nothing in his way, took a single step, tripped, and immediately fell to his knees.

"Rus?"

He forced himself up. Though faint, the voice was unmistakable. Jodie! He'd never felt so pleased to hear his cousin. "Right here!" he shouted.

"Where are you?"

Following her voice, Rus eased himself through the forest to the plane.

"What are you *doing*?" she asked as he drew near.

"Just—" he told her, thinking fast, *"you* know— taking a leak."

7

Jodie cried off and on all night, embarrassed to be so upset but unable to control herself. She couldn't believe how miserable she felt—sweaty, sore, and itchy all over. The leaf-strewn dirt was rough and prickly. She couldn't relax enough to doze off no matter what position she tried. And the bugs! Scratching, brushing, swatting, even hitting her own arms and legs and chest, Jodie tried to repel the invaders but failed over and over until her annoyance, pain, sadness, and frustration left her sobbing.

"Knock it off!" Rus yelled at her repeatedly. "Don't be such a *girl*." As if the bugs weren't bad enough, she had to tolerate her cousin's taunts.

But in one respect Jodie felt reassured by these obnoxious words. They proved that Rus was still there. Throughout the night she had worried that he might try sneaking off; at one point she thought he'd actually left. It turned out he'd only stepped away to pee. Now she felt better about his intentions.

Was night ending? She couldn't tell. Somehow the forest seemed lighter now. Even so, she couldn't see any individual trees or the plane or even Rus and Matt, who must have been just a few feet away. Everything was a tangle of shadows.

What definitely changed was what she heard. All night long the insect sounds had reached her. Hums. Whines. Stutters and clicks. Now, little by little, strange cries started up all around. A few seemed innocent and familiar—cheeps, chirps, twitters—just like birds back home. Other noises were almost comically strange. One sounded like someone blowing across an empty soda bottle. Another resembled the *creak. . . creak. . . creak . . .* of a badly oiled teeter-totter. Another sounded like the clatter of someone running a stick along a picket fence. Another seemed identical to the *brrrrrt?* of a thumb strumming a comb. *Who-hoe!* something called out on her right. *Who-hoe! Who-hoe! Who-hoe!*

Heard one by one, these noises spooked her; jumbled together, they drove her half-crazy with alarm. What could be making such odd racket? Fierce animals? Birds? Jodie pictured vultures lurking in the trees. They wouldn't attack her. . . would they?

Dazed, she listened for a long time. The forest all around grew lighter; she could soon make out individual trees, branches, even leaves. She saw her brother and her cousin nearby. And though she ached from the weight of her fatigue and from the still greater weight of the situation she faced, Jodie couldn't help but feel cheered by the sight of daylight seeping into the forest.

Matt had never felt anything like the hunger he felt on waking up that morning. Hunger so sharp that his stomach throbbed like a wound. Hunger so deep that his whole body felt buzzy and numb. Hunger so intense that he couldn't think about anything but hunger.

"Rus?" Matt said to his cousin where he lay just a short distance to his left.

"What."

"I need some food."

"So? Join the club," Rus answered without moving.

Matt couldn't see his expression. Rus didn't sound angry, just tired. "I was wondering," Matt continued, "if you'd loan me some candy."

"Loan you some?"

"Well, *you* know." Matt forced a laugh.

Rus didn't answer.

Then Jodie said, "Come on, Rus, don't be greedy."

"Greedy!" Rus exclaimed. He sat up suddenly. "Did I hear you right? You guys ate your stuff yesterday,

34

and I saved mine, and you want *my* share, but *I'm* the one who's greedy!" Ducking to avoid the plane's tail overhead, Rus crawled onto open ground, stood, and stretched. His hair stuck out sideways from the left side of his head. Bug bites speckled his face. Eight or ten long, bloody scratches streaked his left arm.

"It's only fair," Matt said. He braced himself for another squabble.

But Rus didn't argue. He only glanced at Matt and Jodie, then walked off, heading toward the river.

Matt's eyes welled up with tears. He missed his parents. Mom, especially. Was it really possible that he'd been with her just a little more than a day earlier? She had fixed them a dinner of chili dogs, french fries, cole slaw, and chocolate pudding. Matt had devoured the food—his favorite meal—and asked her, "What's the food like in Peru?" She'd answered, "Oh, quite a bit different for the Peruvians, but most of the medical folks eat regular gringo food." *Gringo food.* Gringos, Matt knew, were Americans. He felt pleased to know there'd be gringo food. But right now the memories of chili dogs and french fries, and of Mom serving them, hurt so badly that he winced. Would he ever get back home? Would he ever sit at the kitchen table while dinner cooked on the stove and he hung out with Mom and Dad?

"Matt."

He felt Jodie's hand on his shoulder. "What," he said, shrugging it off.

"We'll find something to eat," she reassured him. "I promise."

"Sure," Matt said. "Lots of stuff grows in the jungle." When he looked around, though, all he could see was leaves, leaves, and more leaves.

Waves of sadness and confusion washed over him. He couldn't imagine how he'd ever survive long enough for anyone to get him out of this strange, terrifying place and take him home.

* * *

Nibbling M&Ms, Rus wandered along the river-bank. Grasses, weeds, and little bushes grew almost all the way down to the water's edge. The bank itself, made of gray-brown clay, was dense and slippery. The river flowed two, maybe three miles per hour. Across the river, a wall of green rose above the opposite bank. Overhead a flock of small red and blue birds flew by, squawking, in a big hurry. A dragonfly hovered for a moment right ahead of him and zipped away.

He picked up a stick, threw it hard, and watched it arc. It splashed feebly and sent out a few ripples. Light twisted on the river.

Where, Rus asked himself, could you get a decent meal around here? Even a snack? He'd thought that in the rainforest, fruit would dangle from every branch: bananas, pears, mangoes, bright squishy things. Not exactly his favorite foods, but Rus wasn't picky. Anything would do. He'd eat whatever would help him survive.

Rus popped more M&Ms into his mouth. They tasted painfully good. His mouth felt so electric that he imagined sparks flying off his face as he chewed.

It was just as well, he decided, that his escape plan had failed the night before. The jungle looked even denser than he'd first thought; even by daylight he found it hard to walk more than twenty feet without getting lost. He wouldn't have gotten far alone. Still, he felt more and more concerned about being stuck in the jungle.

Physical discomforts weren't really what worried him. He'd roughed it before. Even when Mom had earned enough bucks to rent an apartment, things hadn't been exactly posh. They'd lived one winter in a totally unfurnished apartment. No tables, chairs, sofas, beds. There was a fridge but no electricity. There was a stove but no gas. They slept on the floor and kept warm by using their coats as blankets. They ate cold meals—soup,

36

beans, beef stew—right out of the cans. Sometimes they didn't eat at all. They managed. Rus knew he could sweat through a few days here, too.

But what if no one comes? he wondered. What if they waited and waited but no one found them? The rainforest was huge. From the air, Rus had seen how it stretched clear to the horizon, an expanse of trees interrupted only by a web of rivers. Even well-organized search parties might succeed in covering only a fraction of the terrain.

He raised the little brown bag of M&Ms and let a bunch more slide, clicking, into his mouth. It was a good thing he'd claimed his share of the candy; Rus couldn't even guess when they'd find something else to eat.

He swiveled suddenly to face the Badger. A path of smashed little trees and torn-up vegetation led forty or fifty feet from the riverbank to where the plane had come to rest. He could see the battered fuselage easily from his vantage point. But how would it look from above? In crash-landing, the plane had skidded into the forest and burrowed in among the trees. The wings had mowed down lots of saplings near the riverbank, but several bigger trees had stopped the Badger in a way that left it engulfed in foliage. If Rus had wanted to hide a plane on purpose—maybe covering it with camouflage netting, like in the movies—he couldn't have hidden it better than what had happened by accident.

8

W<i>here are the people?</i> Jodie wondered as she explored the area surrounding the crash site. <i>Where are the Indians who live here?</i>

For that whole first morning after the crash, Jodie wandered near the wreckage with her brother and her cousin, she walked up along the riverbank, and she watched and listened to the sights and sounds around them. They saw and heard no human beings except each other.

"Hey!" Jodie yelled, standing by the water. "Somebody? *Help* us!"

No one answered.

The silence made no sense. The Amazonian rainforest, as Jodie had learned from her father's stories, supported a large human population. Indians had lived in the forest for thousands of years. According to Dad, most tribes had kept to themselves for centuries, and many had lived in nearly complete isolation from the outside world. This situation had been changing over the past few decades. Outsiders had made contact with most of the Indians. Many tribes had emerged from the remote forest areas, shed their old customs, acquired new ones, and started living a more modern way of life. There ought to be people nearby, Jodie told herself.

"Hey! Somebody!" she hollered.

A bird across the river called back: *"Aw!"*

So after years of hearing Dad's stories about life in the rainforest, Jodie knew that this place wasn't a wilderness. Even the less densely settled places had people living here and there. Few parts of the forest were uninhabited.

But where were the people?

Then, abruptly, two human voices:

38

"—so *stop* it, would you?"

"No, *you* stop it!"

Jodie walked down the riverbank, away from the boys.

She felt increasingly alarmed about their situation. They had drunk plenty of water from one of the big plastic jugs but they hadn't eaten any food since the night before. They had seen no rescue planes. They had done nothing to improve their chances of getting out of there alive. All three of them felt awful—weak, achy, and sick. The heat and humidity made Jodie so nauseated that she worried almost constantly about throwing up. Her skin itched from dozens of insect bites.

"That's not what I said!" Matt hollered from somewhere in the forest.

As wearisome as she found her brother and her cousin, she suddenly wanted nothing more than to be with them. Anything to avoid being alone.

Scrambling up the riverbank, she glanced back toward the water and the forest rising beyond it. What was there, she wondered, beyond that green wall?

And *who?*

9

What a creepy place, Matt told himself as he looked for food. The whole forest was berserk with leaves. If he took more than twenty steps in any direction, he couldn't spot Rus or Jodie. He wanted to return to the crash site but couldn't remember the way back. When he noticed a rustling noise, he stopped abruptly. Something was following him. There: beyond a wall-like tangle of palm leaves.

Matt held his breath. *Lions and tigers and bears, oh my!*

He didn't know whether to scream or hide or run away. Matt stood there shaking as the animal pushed through the foliage, closer and closer. . .

"Hi there."

It was Jodie! Watching her ease past a gap in the bushes, Matt didn't know whether to hug her—or slug her. "Don't *do* that!" he hollered.

"Do what?"

"Scare me to death!"

"Serves you right," she said, annoyed. "Don't walk off without telling me."

"Yes, Mother."

"What are you doing, anyway?"

Matt shrugged. "Looking for food," he told her. "And getting away from Rus."

"Me too. What a pain in the neck."

He felt pleased to hear his sister speak about Rus that way. Matt knew that Jodie didn't like their cousin, but sometimes he wondered how much she liked *Matt* anymore. She acted so stuck up when all three of them were together. Sometimes she refused to talk with them. Sometimes she pretended they didn't even exist. Now, at least for a moment, things seemed more like how they used to be.

"Let's forget about Rus," Jodie said. "What matters is something to eat."

"You think there's food here?"

"There's gotta be." Jodie started looking this way and that, scanning the trees.

Matt gazed upward, too. Surely some kind of fruit grew here, just waiting to be picked and eaten. He imagined finding a whole bunch of ripe bananas. . .

"Look at those!" Jodie shouted suddenly. "Right overhead!"

He tried to see what she pointed to. There! Some dark brown things. Not too high, maybe ten or twelve feet up a skinny little tree.

"Coconuts!" he yelled.

"They're not coconuts," Jodie told him. "They're way too small."

At once she raced over to the tree and started to climb. Matt wasn't surprised: Jodie liked climbing trees and did it well. He'd never been able to keep up with her, and he'd always resented her ability. When Rus moved in, Matt had enjoyed hearing their cousin tease her. *"Tomboy!"* Rus would holler whenever Jodie scrambled up a tree. Right now Matt didn't care as long as she brought down some food.

Jodie pulled herself about five feet up the narrow tree trunk, then lost her footing. She clung there, hollered once—"Get back!"—and crashed to the ground.

"You okay?" Matt asked, rushing over.

She lay on her side a few moments before sitting up. "I guess so."

Matt looked around. Along with lots of leaves, many dead branches lay on the ground. Most of them weren't very long. Could he invent something to help reach those brown things? He stooped, picked up two long sticks, and examined them. Matt noticed some

41

stringy vines, too, dangling from a nearby tree. Maybe he could make this stuff into a grabber.

"What are you doing?" Jodie asked, rubbing her left hip.

"Just messing around."

Working fast, Matt lay the sticks on the ground. He placed them with their ends overlapping by about six inches, then tied them together with a length of stringy vine. The vines were stiffer than he'd expected but worked well enough to bind the sticks. Rus would tease him—he'd call him Professor Invento—but Matt's new device would harvest delicious fruit right off the tree. Matt to the rescue!

He raised the grabber, touching those brown fruits easily.

"Way to go!" Jodie shouted.

"Yay!" Matt exclaimed. "I think I've got it!"

What were they, anyway? Seed pods? The grabber swayed in his hands. Sweating hard, Matt swung, trying to knock the pod off the tree. He missed. Then, suddenly, Matt struck hard enough that the grabber knocked the pods loose. They dropped, striking the ground just a few feet away from where he stood.

"Yes!" Jodie yelled, leaping into the air.

They raced over to what had fallen.

"Lunch time!" Matt hollered, snatching up the pods, and he raced off.

Rus listened to his cousins and tried to stay patient. Matt had apparently invented some sort of goofy device for grabbing stuff. They'd used it to pick some fruit. Now they could feast all day! They'd have a five-course dinner! "All right!" Rus shouted. "Enough babbling—just show me the goods."

Matt, hiding something behind his back, suddenly held it out. "Look at this!"

What Rus saw didn't quite make sense. Potatoes? No, too small and egg-shaped. Kiwi fruit? Maybe—they were brown and woody-looking. But when Rus took them from Matt, they felt too dense and heavy.

Jodie said, "Let's eat!"

Rus couldn't help laughing. "Eat *this?* It's hard as a rock!"

"So crack it open!" Matt yelled, jumping up and down in excitement.

"Here," Jodie said, grabbing at the cluster.

"Hey! Hands off!" Rus snapped. When his cousins finally pulled back, he succeeded in ripping one of the pods off the cluster. He examined it for cracks but found no way to pry it open. Then he reached over to the plane, rubbed the pod against some torn metal, and scraped away the outer husk.

Matt shoved his face closer. "What's inside?"

Under the husk was a reddish-brown layer of wet fuzz. Rus looked at it uneasily. It looked bizarre, but he felt so hungry that he couldn't resist trying it. He brought the pod up to his mouth and took a bite.

At once he gagged. Never in his life had Rus tasted anything so bitter. His tongue tightened and his throat constricted. Rus threw the pod down and spat on the ground over and over.

"Not your favorite?" Jodie asked, chuckling.

Rus stopped hawking long enough to glare at her. "Laugh all you want."

He expected her to stomp off, but she didn't. Instead, she picked up the pod, looked around, and set it on a fallen log. "Maybe the good part is inside," she said. Jodie grabbed a stick and, striking with a sudden *thwack*, split the pod in two.

Matt scrambled to grab one of the halves. "Look!" he hollered. "It's—"

43

"Give it." Rus snatched the pod from his cousin, who handed it over without resistance. Surely there would be something edible. . .

He stared at the husk in his hands.

Tiny white worms writhed inside a tangle of slimy-looking fibers.

Close to vomiting, Rus threw the pod into the forest with all his might. "Great," he told the others. "This won't do. We've got to try harder."

Jodie and Matt, sitting under the plane's tail, stared if he'd suggested walking to the moon. "I'm too tired," Matt complained, "and too hungry."

Rus slapped his thighs in exasperation. "Isn't that the point? You're such spoiled brats! You think food's just gonna fall right into your hands?"

"But this is the rainforest!" Jodie whined. "It's supposed to be *full* of food."

Rus huffed loudly. "Well, maybe I'm just blind."

Jodie shrugged. "Maybe we don't *need* any food. We'll get rescued—"

"There's a one percent chance anyone'll find us," he told her, and he explained what concerned him. Maybe a rescue plane would spot them. Maybe a boat would come up the river. Maybe a search party would push its way through the forest. But maybe not. So far they hadn't seen or heard a single plane or boat or even another human being. It seemed idiotic just to wait. Getting rescued might not happen for a while. Even a few days' wait would leave them desperate with hunger. And it was possible that rescuers might not find them at all. "So we have to help them," Rus explained. "We have to meet them halfway."

"Yeah, but how?" Matt asked.

"That's what we have to figure out."

"I know!" Jodie exclaimed. "We could write a note, stick it in one of our canteens, and float it down the river. Then someone'll come rescue us."

"Yeah, right," Rus responded with a laugh. "If anyone even spots it."

Matt said, "And besides, we wouldn't know how to tell people where we are."

"Good point," Rus said.

They sat there a while without speaking. Rus felt something on his ankle: tiny red ants! He brushed them off, then scratched furiously as the itching spread.

"Hey!" Matt shouted. "We could make a boat!"

"A boat?" Jodie asked.

"Sure! We could take some metal from the wreck, make it into a boat, and float down the river." Matt looked so pleased with himself.

Rus felt totally fed up. He hadn't expected much from Jodie and Matt, but he'd never thought their suggestions would be so lame. "Great," he said. "I'll just pull an acetylene torch out of my back pocket and set to work." He faked a grin. "And while we're at it, why settle for a boat? Why not a cabin cruiser! A yacht! An ocean liner!"

Matt glared at him. "It was just an idea."

"A dumb idea," Rus said.

"Hey—he's doing his best," Jodie scolded.

"Which isn't too great, is it?"

"It's better than *your* ideas," she told Rus. "Where's *your* brainstorms?"

They sat in silence. Rus considered prodding them but felt too tired to bother. Just sitting there with Professor Invento and the Princess weighed him down. They were like a—what was it Mom sometimes called him?—a millstone. Whatever that was. Obviously something heavy. *You're a millstone around my neck,* she'd say when she was drunk. Jodie and Matt were millstones, too. What Rus had hoped would lighten his load now made it feel much heavier instead.

Before he could speak, though, something startled him: rain. There was no transition. One moment the air was dry; the next, it was dense with rain. Rus could scarcely see the opposite riverbank. Even Jodie, sitting five feet away, looked fuzzy from all the water between them. The noise was terrific.

All three of them scurried under the plane's tail, but within a few seconds they were drenched. What had seemed a hot day soon felt chilly. Rus crouched, trying to make himself a small target, but it didn't help, and within minutes he started shivering uncontrollably.

Jodie sat in the wrecked Badger and stared through the oval window as the rain poured down. She hated being on board the plane—a bad musty odor had started to come from up front—but at the moment she preferred being there to getting soaked. She couldn't believe how heavily the rain fell. Even hiding under the tail hadn't kept them dry. They would spend only enough time on the plane for the storm to ease.

Crouched in the same seat she'd sat in during the flight, Jodie said, "Rus is right—we have to do something. But we won't know *what*," she continued, "till we know what we have to work with."

Rus, slouched in his seat across the aisle, sat up. "What are you getting at?"

"Let's size up our stuff and decide what we can do."

"And invent something!" Matt exclaimed.

So they all rummaged through the plane and noted anything useful. They checked the storage compartments. They looked under the seats. They searched through whatever the pilots had stowed on board. Other than some boxes of medical supplies and the kids' own day packs, though, the Badger was almost empty.

"What about the cargo hold?" Matt asked. "You know—under the plane."

"I already thought of that," Rus said. "Maybe there's stuff inside. But we'll never know because the plane crashed with the landing gear up. The wreck is resting belly-down on the cargo door. We'll never get it open."

"Great," Jodie muttered, feeling more and more disappointed.

"What we've got is what's right here."

Writing on a scrap of paper she'd found in the plane, Jodie made a list:

> 3 small day packs
> 2 1-liter water bottles
> 2 extra T-shirts (M's and J's)
> 1 pair extra shorts (J's)
> Some candy bars (R's)
> 6 big plastic jugs—full of water
> 1 roll wide clear plastic sheet
> Uncertain amount of wire (from wreckage)
> 12 boxes assorted medical suture kits
> 12 boxes assorted disposable scalpel blades
> 1 box scalpel handles
> 100 pairs surgical gloves
> 1 roll tourniquet rubber
> 1000 misc. band aids
> 10 boxes misc. surgical tape

She felt shocked by how little they had to work with. No food except for Rus's candy. Almost no clothing. No tools, unless you counted the scalpel blades. Just a few other odds and ends. That was it.

"Great!" Rus exclaimed, opening a box. "Band aids!"

"Oh, *stop*," Jodie grumbled.

He held up a fistful of band aids. "We can get cut a thousand times and we'll be just fine. That's three hundred thirty-three cuts apiece."

"It's not funny," she said.

"Who said it's funny? Band aids are just what I need." Rus showed off the scratches on his left arm.

47

"Gross!" Matt exclaimed. "How'd you get cut so bad?"

"What's it to you?"

Jodie, still shocked by the sight of Rus's wounds, said, "You should take care of those."

As if taunting her, he pulled open wrappers and started to stick band aids on his arm.

How will we get by with so little stuff? Jodie asked herself. Even if a rescue helicopter descended from the sky at that same instant, they were already exhausted, sore, and half-crazed from hunger. And if no one rescued them so soon?

10

Frustrated by their lack of gear, Matt went down to the river. So what if they didn't have enough stuff? He'd invent something anyway, all by himself!

First he found some sticks and set them on the muddy riverbank. They were only a half-inch thick—very green and bendy—and maybe two or three feet long. Matt wondered if they'd float. Tossing a branch into the water, he watched it plop almost without a splash. Within a few minutes it was ten yards downstream.

Matt set ten of the sticks side by side. Then he took some other sticks and wove them in and out among the first set. Sort of like a project he'd done at summer camp: weaving cloth loops into a hot pot holder. This was like weaving, too, only the "cloth" was made of sticks.

"What's this?"

Matt looked up. Rus stood gazing down at him from the riverbank's high rim. "Nothing," Matt answered.

"Your latest ingenious contraption?" Rus asked.

"I'm just messing around."

"Look, I hate to interrupt your brainstorm, but we're in big, big trouble."

"I know that." Matt kept weaving sticks in and out.

"Why are you wasting time like this?"

Matt shrugged.

Rus slid down the bank and looked at the platform. "I just don't believe it!" he shouted suddenly. "If you're gonna do something, go look for food!"

"I already did," Matt hollered, "but you didn't like what I found."

Rus laughed. "Great! So let's give up!" He scrambled up the riverbank.

Suddenly Matt felt ridiculous. He looked at his toy raft and wondered why he'd ever built it. Food: now *that's* what mattered. He picked up the raft and threw it at the river. It landed part way in the water and rested there without moving.

Before Matt could turn to Rus, though, something caught his attention. A noise. Barely audible at first, it soon became a whiny buzz. *Like the Badger,* he thought. And at that moment something flashed overhead, something smaller than he expected but clearly metallic, close enough to drown out the kids' shouts and fast enough that the silence closed in quickly as the airplane disappeared.

The plane didn't come back. It didn't loop around. It didn't waggle its wings to signal Rus and the other kids screaming at it far below. It just flew away.

Rus stood on the riverbank and tried to will it back. He'd concentrate all his mental energy and catch the pilot's attention. He'd force him to change course, swing around, and have another look. *Come back, come back, come back,* Rus chanted under his breath. *Come back, come back.* Just as Rus had exerted his will to keep Mom sober, to land her a job, to find them an apartment, to fight her liver disease—just as he'd done all that, Rus would exert his will again to make the pilot return, notice, and rescue him.

He stood there and waited. He scanned the sky and the tree line. He listened.

Great clouds billowed in the sky.

A white butterfly zigzagged across the water.

A bird called out: *Are you. . . fine?*

"What are we going to do?" Jodie asked Rus.

He shrugged.

"You think they'll fly over us again some day?"

He shrugged again.

50

"They'll rescue us, won't they?" she asked. She didn't want to upset Matt, who stood trembling and weeping a few feet away, but she couldn't restrain herself. "Won't they come rescue us?"

Jodie realized just then that Rus wasn't sure. He looked so discouraged that he didn't—for once—have a snappy comeback. And the thought of Rus feeling so doubtful suddenly terrified her.

"I *hate* this place!" Matt shouted. "I *hate* it!"

Rus and Jodie just stared at him. That made Matt even angrier. "You're the big guys, right? I'm just the stupid eight-year-old! *Right?*" When they still didn't react, Matt kicked a box of medical supplies sitting nearby on the ground.

"You're eight?" Rus asked. "You're acting more like three!"

Matt picked up the box, then threw it down. Band-aids came flying out and scattered on the ground. "I don't care!" he hollered, and he started throwing stuff—packets, boxes, and the roll of plastic. "I hate Peru! I hate the rainforest! I hate both of you!" He kicked a small box, scattering band aids like flower petals, and stomped on them. "I wish I'd never come here, ever!"

He kicked another box, which burst open. Rolls of white tape came flying out, and the rolls bounded away, some going all the way down the bank to the river.

Matt chased after them, kicked them, and slowed only when he reached the water. Then he picked up the raft he'd woven out of sticks, raised it high over his head, and flung it hard. This time it struck the river with a little slapping noise. It lay there a moment before the water began to carry it off.

Stopping short, Matt stared as the raft drifted away.

Of course, he thought. Why hadn't it occurred to him earlier?

11

Rus couldn't believe Matt's latest scheme. "So what you're saying," he said with a laugh, "is you want to float down river on that stupid little thing you made?"

"No, on a *real* raft!" Matt shouted. "*Like* the one I made, only big!"

"Great idea," Rus muttered. "Bring me a chain saw and I'll set to work."

Matt wouldn't give up. "I know what you're thinking. It sounds stupid, right? But we can do it. We'll use the little stuff—branches, sticks, crud like that."

"Saplings," Jodie said. "Baby trees."

"Right," Matt said.

"This is nuts!" Rus hollered. "It's dumb."

Before he could say more, Jodie came at him, pointing her finger like a knife. "Hey! *You're* the one who said we have to rescue ourselves, so let's do it."

"It's totally dumb," Rus protested.

"It's not!" Matt shouted.

"If you don't like it," Jodie told Rus, "then what's *your* idea? Huh?"

Rus, resenting Jodie's attempt to pin him down, refused to answer.

She smiled her most annoying *gotcha!* smile. "Just as I thought. All right—let's listen to Matt. I'm not saying his idea will work, but let's hear him out."

Rus wanted to object—he hated how this sassy girl lectured him—but he started to feel curious about how Matt would explain himself. "Okay, Professor. You think you're so great at inventing things? Prove it."

So Matt babbled away without making much sense. Rus struggled to stay patient. What were the chances that an eight-year-old would solve their problem? His ridicu-

52

lous plan would just make things worse. Still, Rus listened. It seemed easier to pay attention than to get in a fight by ignoring him.

"We'll kinda weave some sticks together—you know, *big* sticks—practically poles, or something. That'll make a platform. . ."

Matt explained that they could build a raft out of skinny trees and branches that the Badger had cut down when it crashed. Assuming it held together, Rus, Jodie, and Matt could ride it downstream. Matt claimed to have seen some towns near a river shortly before the plane crashed, so maybe they could float far enough to reach civilization. It would take them a few days, maybe even a week, but they'd be better off that way than waiting and waiting for a rescue that might never happen.

Matt finished explaining his plan and stood there grinning like someone who'd just won the lottery. "So—what d'you think?"

"I think we should try it," Jodie announced.

Rus wanted to say, *Don't be ridiculous*, but he didn't. Throwing together a raft from bits of junk didn't seem likely to work, but just sitting there—bored, tired, and hungry—would be unbearable.

He looked around. The sun had already slipped behind the far wall of trees. Clouds overhead glowed silvery gold. "It'll be dark soon," Rus told his cousins.

"Tomorrow, then," Jodie said. "First thing."

"Yay!" Matt yelled. "We're going home!"

Could they really reach a town or city downstream? Rus felt scared to do what his cousins suggested and equally scared to pass up the chance. Would this crazy plan give them their best shot at survival? Or maybe rule it out altogether?

"Come *on*," Jodie nagged him.

Rus shoved his fingers through his hair. He couldn't think of any alternative.

"Okay," he said. "Let's give it a shot."

12

The next morning, as they carried their supplies down to the riverbank, Jodie felt more and more intrigued by Matt's idea, but she also worried about the risks involved. The possibility of rafting down the river delighted her. They'd leave the wrecked Badger behind! They'd float to safety! They'd be with Dad in no time! Yet as she thought through the plan more closely, she couldn't help but wonder if the raft was really such a good idea. Weren't you supposed to stay put when lost? You didn't go wandering off—that made the rescuers' job more difficult. You waited to be found. That's what her parents had taught her back in New Jersey.

Still, this situation wasn't like any she'd ever discussed with Mom and Dad. It wasn't as if she'd wandered off a trail while hiking in the local nature preserve. This was the Peruvian rainforest. Who could say when the rescuers would show up? What if the kids waited by the plane but no one found them? Lugging stuff down to the river, Jodie flip-flopped from one worry to the next.

Nearing the plane at one point, something reminded her of how much was at stake. That smell. . . That sharp, repulsive smell. Even the tiniest whiff made her gag. She felt a deep disgust at the thought of the pilots' bodies still trapped in the wreckage. But at once she felt something even stronger: fear. *Get away!* a voice shouted from deep inside her mind. *Get away—or you'll end up just like them!*

So it wasn't hard to keep moving, to do whatever seemed necessary, to give Matt's idea every possible chance of working.

"Okay, Professor," Rus said once they'd brought everything down to the river. "What's the first step?"

"A platform," Matt replied. "Like what I made the other day out of sticks."

Rus laughed harshly. "Sticks! Great—as long as we shrink to six inches tall."

"Not a *small* platform!" Matt shouted. "A *big* one! Made of *big* branches—"

"Wood from the trees!" Jodie exclaimed. A tangle of vines, branches, and even whole saplings lay at their feet. "Look at this—all the wood we'd ever want."

It didn't take long for the kids to pick out what they needed. They set twenty-five pole-like branches in a row, each branch about two or three inches from the ones right next to it, and they made another row, crosswise, to form a grid.

"That looks pretty good," Matt said.

"Don't get too excited," Rus warned him. "How'll you hook 'em together?"

"Wire," Matt suggested.

"*Wire?*" Rus asked, frowning.

"Sure—wire from the plane."

"What a dumb idea."

"It's not so dumb," Jodie stated. "First of all, there's lots of wire hanging out of the wreckage, so let's use it. Second, lots of things get hooked up with wire."

Rus looked more and more annoyed. "Like what?"

She just smiled, revealing the braces on her teeth.

He turned away in annoyance. "Wonderful. I'm sure if it works on teeth it'll be just great on a raft."

Jodie didn't bother to explain. She simply set to work. She took a length of wire, wound it several times around the place where two branches crossed, then twisted the ends together. The result was wobbly, but the joint held. "See?"

The wire worked well enough—until they ran out. By the time they'd used up their whole supply, they had secured only about two thirds of the branches that needed to be joined. The rest remained unattached.

"So much for wire," Rus said gloomily.

"There's more on the plane," Jodie told him.

But getting it turned out to be too difficult. The Badger must have had miles of wire inside its crumpled body, yet most of it was still encased in metal, plastic, or both. The kids' efforts to pull some wire loose yielded only a few more feet.

Jodie watched Rus. She could tell that he wanted to drop the whole plan. Before he could speak, she said, "We'll try something else."

"Great," he replied gloomily. "Like what?"

Matt, Rus, and Jodie looked around as if something would fall from the sky.

No one spoke for a long time.

Then Matt shouted, "I know—those stringy vines!"

"*Vines?*" Rus sneered as he spoke.

"I used them on my grabber. The stuff's like rope but grows on trees."

Jodie thought vines might work, so she set off at once, looking for the right thickness. Within a few minutes, she'd found several long strands.

It was trickier to use than she'd expected. Some of the strands were so dry that they splintered like pencils. Others were too thin and snapped as easily as string. Still others worked out well enough but took a long time to tie properly.

"This is the pits!" Jodie hollered after several hours of work. "At this rate, it'll be days before we finish."

"I told you the plan was a dud," Rus announced.

"You got a better idea?" Matt asked.

"No—but what could be worse than yours?"

Jodie's spirits sank. Her hands, scraped by handling the vines, stung badly. She looked around, walked over to one of the boxes of medical supplies, and started to rummage around. She pulled out a gauze pad and a roll of adhesive tape. Sitting down, she started to tape a bandage across her left palm.

"That's it!" Matt said suddenly.

"*Now* what?" Rus grumbled.

"Tape!"

Jodie understood him at once. "We'll *tape* the branches together."

"Why not?" Matt asked. "It's strong stuff. It's easy to use. And we've got piles and piles of it."

By late afternoon, they'd finished. The rain disrupted them at one point—a shower so intense that it drenched the kids and even washed some packets of medical supplies halfway down the riverbank to the river. They gathered up their goods, though, and hid aboard the foul-smelling plane till the downpour eased. Then, soaked but not discouraged, they finished lashing the poles, sticks, and saplings together. The result looked fairly strong. To secure it further, the kids took some of the clear plastic from the roll they'd found on the plane and taped it on top of the platform. This strengthened the whole structure and, best of all, created a crude floor they could sit on.

"Well, there it is," Matt announced.

"Sure is ugly," Rus said.

Jodie groaned. "Can't you say *anything* positive?"

"Not when I'm looking at *this* piece of junk."

"It doesn't matter how it looks," Matt said. "Only how it floats."

"It won't last half an hour," Rus announced.

Matt smiled at his invention. "I bet it will."

"Bet it won't."

"Then *you* figure out something better," Jodie dared her cousin.

Rus stood staring at the raft. "All right, all right—let's see if it works."

13

Matt grabbed one end of the raft and tugged. It was heavier than he'd expected. He could barely drag it, and lifting wasn't even a possibility. That worried him—a raft was supposed to be light. Worried about straining himself, he called out to Jodie and Rus: "Aren't you gonna help?"

Jodie came over and pitched in next to Matt. Rus lifted the other end. Grunting, they carried the raft eight or ten feet to the river, placed one side in the water, and shoved the other side until the whole thing rested on the surface.

"It floats!" Matt yelled with pride and relief when he saw that his idea had succeeded. "It really floats!"

"Yes!" Jodie shouted, shoving her fist upward.

Rus said, "Not so fast. The big question is, will it keep *us* afloat?"

As the raft drifted slowly near the shore, the kids walked along the clay bank. Matt worried that the raft might escape, so he hurried ahead. Before it could get away, though, Jodie pulled off her sneakers, waded into the river, and caught hold of the platform. The water came up to her knees. She turned her back to the raft, then sat down. The raft tilted slightly, letting water slide onto the clear plastic floor.

"Uh-oh," Rus said.

"Hop on board," Jodie told him. "Let's see what happens."

Matt pulled off his shoes and stepped into the water, then hesitated. "Wait! What if there's—what are those fish called? The ones that bite?"

"Piranhas," Jodie answered.

"What if they're in there?"

"Don't worry," said Jodie. "I read somewhere that they won't bite you unless you're already wounded."

Matt felt terrified. What was lurking in that muddy water? "I'm not going in."

"Come on," Rus groaned, "let's get this over with."

Forcing himself, Matt stepped carefully into the river. The water felt almost warm. Mud squished between his toes. He flinched, waiting for the first bite.

Nothing happened.

Matt reached the raft and struggled to push himself on board. He couldn't believe how weak he felt. After two tries, though, he succeeded. His weight pushed that side of the raft slightly beneath the surface. Water sloshed over his legs all the way up to his knees.

Then Rus came over and crawled aboard, too. Once again the raft sank further. Soon one whole side of it was at least four inches under water.

Matt felt so discouraged that he couldn't even talk. "Well—" he said, then fell silent. His invention was a total failure.

Rus eased off the raft and splashed to shore. "Look at the bright side," he stated irritably, "we're not eating much these days, are we? Maybe we'll lose so much weight that even *this* worthless thing will keep us afloat." Streaming water, Rus climbed up the riverbank and headed for the plane.

Jodie slid off the raft, grabbed it, and towed it to shore. Matt watched her from where he sat. Stunned with embarrassment and fear, he couldn't move. She reached out to help him off. "It's okay," she said in a sugary voice.

"No, it's *not!*" Matt yelled, ignoring Jodie's hand. "It's *not* okay!" He staggered through the water till he reached the shore.

"You tried, Matt."

"Just leave me alone." He shoved past her and ran into the forest.

14

S unset. The sky became a furnace: the clouds pulsed yellow-orange, subsided red as embers, then cooled ash-gray. Night fell quickly.

Fed up and exhausted, Rus avoided his cousins. He couldn't believe he'd wasted so much time on Matt's ridiculous raft. A whole day down the drain! Now they were even more tired, sore, bug-bitten, and hungry than before. Not to mention grouchy. As the day ended, he did everything possible to stay clear of them.

What were they going to do? Rus had almost believed they could really build a raft. The plan wasn't as stupid as he'd first thought. A raft capable of supporting more weight might have worked. The only hitch was the lack of tools; if they'd had even a single ax, they could have chopped down real trees and made a bigger platform. The diddly branches they'd used wouldn't keep even a single kid afloat, much less three.

But if they didn't have a raft, how would they survive? No rescuers had showed up, and hiking out would be suicide. Rus felt more and more trapped. This wasn't as simple as a computer game, he noted—he couldn't just hit Command-Q or ESC to bail out.

Wandering among the trees, Rus poked at the leaves in hopes of finding food. Nuts, roots, berries: anything to ease the fire in his belly. He found nothing.

"I'm thirsty"—that was Matt's whiny voice somewhere close to the plane.

"So drink," Jodie told him.

Rus wouldn't be able to ignore his cousins any longer; he'd have to face the inevitable and go back to the plane. It wasn't just Matt and Jodie whose company he dreaded. The pilots, too. . . The stench aboard the Badger was now unbearable, and not just because of the odor itself. Smelling it, Rus thought at once of his mother, of what had happened to her, and at once his mood dropped even further.

He went down to the riverbank to avoid Jodie and Matt for a few more minutes. He watched the river for a while. Gray light twisted on the surface. Hundreds of bugs zipped about on the water. Thousands more billowed in the air. Rus felt too exhausted to swat them when they landed on his skin.

He took a stick and started writing in the mud.

ALICE

Thinking about Mom tensed him up. He missed her, yet he resented missing her more than he really missed her. How could he miss a mother who didn't take care of him? Who cared more about drinking booze than about feeding her own son? Who neglected him so much that he went to school infested with bugs?

Rus rubbed out the A.

LICE

It was enough to leave him feeling cold even in the jungle. He rubbed out the L.

ICE

And who did that leave him counting on? Rus smudged out the C and the E:

I

15

Crouched on the ground, Jodie looked up when Rus returned to the plane. She had been pouring water from one of the big jugs into Matt's plastic canteen. Even if she couldn't feed her brother, she could at least keep him from getting dehydrated. He didn't look so great—droopy, pale, and speckled with bloody bug bites. He looked sad, too: now he blamed himself for the failure of the raft! It bothered Jodie that he'd take it so personally.

"Having a bedtime snack?" Rus asked.

She ignored him.

"We should count ourselves lucky," Rus went on. He sat nearby on the ground. "At least we have lots of good, nutritious water."

"Please don't bother us," Jodie said, forcing herself to sound polite.

"We can eat anything we want so long as it's water."

"Go away," Matt said weakly.

"Boiled water. Fried water. Barbecued water."

"Look, we're disappointed, too," Jodie said, "but we tried, didn't we?"

"Water stew with water dumplings," Rus said.

"At least we tried."

"Roast water with water gravy and all the watery trimmings."

A huge weight descended on her. How would they ever get home? "Trying is what matters," Jodie insisted. Against her will, she started to cry.

Rus lost his temper. "No, it's *not* what matters!" he shouted suddenly. "Trying isn't what matters. This isn't the sixth grade swim team—it's *life!* This is the real thing!"

Jodie gritted her teeth. She wouldn't let Rus get to her.

"Surviving is what matters!" Rus hollered.

"It's not my fault!" Matt wailed suddenly.

"Oh, stop it," Rus snapped. "Nobody said it's your fault. You're so pathetic it can't be your fault."

This was more than Jodie could tolerate. "Leave him alone!"

Rus laughed at her. "You're pathetic, too."

"Stop it!"

"Both of you are just pathetic."

"Go away!"

"Don't you think I would if I could?" Rus asked angrily. "Don't you think I'd rather be anywhere else but here? Anywhere but with *you?*" Rus kicked out with his right foot, striking the jug, which toppled over. Water gushed out. "With your stinking family?"

Jodie suddenly felt afraid. Standing, she blurted, "Don't you threaten us!"

"*Threaten* you?"

"Don't you dare!"

"Hey, just chill out," Rus said, forcing a laugh.

But Jodie didn't trust him. He wasn't one of them. He never was and never would be. He was a Cooper but not a Cooper. What could her parents have had in mind, adopting this guy? Backing off, Jodie stooped and picked up a stick. Her own actions scared her, menacing Rus like that, but Jodie couldn't restrain herself. "I hate you!" Jodie yelled. "I hate you and I wish you'd never joined our family!"

Rus looked startled. Jodie couldn't make sense of his expression—was that fear on his face? Anger? Sadness? He picked up the plastic jug at his feet, let the remaining water gush out, and held out the container like a shield.

Which Jodie then struck. *Thunk!*

She didn't even swing that hard. She didn't mean to hurt him—she just couldn't control herself. Somehow this whole mess was Rus's fault. *Thunk!*

If only he'd never joined the family. She cried, "You're not my brother!" She swung again. *Thunk!*

If only he'd gone somewhere else to live. "You're not even my cousin!" *Thunk!*

"Put that stick down," Rus told her.

"You're nothing!" *Thunk!*

"Jodie, stop it."

She felt scared that Rus might hit back, but he didn't. He didn't even yell at her. He simply stared and stared. She yelled, "You don't even exist!" *Thunk!*

"Hey! Listen!"

"I won't!"

"No, listen!"

Gradually she realized that Matt, not Rus, was the person shouting. Her brother was hollering, waving, and shaking hard. "You guys, *listen* to me!"

Jodie stared at him, then at her cousin. She let the stick fall from her hand.

Rus lowered the jug.

They looked at one another, confused. Even in the dim twilight, Jodie could tell that all of them felt ridiculous. But suddenly Matt was the center of attention. "I figured it out!" he yelled.

Jodie and Rus exchanged glances.

"Figured *what* out?" Rus asked.

"The raft."

"What are you talking about?" Jodie asked.

Matt thumped the jug still in Rus's hands. "It's so simple!"

16

Matt explained that he'd somehow flipped a switch in his own head. First things seemed one way; then, without warning, they seemed totally different. "I was watching you guys hassle each other," he explained. "Rus picked up that jug. Water came out. Suddenly the jug changed into a shield!"

"And?" Rus said, sounding impatient.

"And—Jodie hit the jug with her stick. Thump!" Matt shouted. "The jug changed into a drum!"

Jodie asked, "What are you getting at?"

"Thump! The jug changed again!"

"I don't get it," Rus said.

"Jugs are hollow." Matt couldn't believe they didn't understand.

"So?" Jodie's voice sounded flat, baffled.

"Hollow things *float*," Matt stated.

Now Jodie and Rus stared at each other.

"Pontoons!" Jodie whispered.

Rus hesitated, then said, "Yeah. Yeah, maybe you're right—pontoons."

"You guys are so dense," Matt said, delighted that they'd finally caught on. "We'll strap them onto the raft!"

17

Rus slept very little that night. Though exhausted, he kept waking up whenever he thought about Matt's new idea. Would it work? Would plastic jugs really keep the raft afloat? It seemed like a great solution to the problem. Of course, the original idea had seemed good, too, but the raft had been a complete flop.

All three kids had wanted to experiment with the jugs that evening. Oddly, Matt had been the person who convinced Rus and Jodie to be patient. "It's nearly dark," he'd said, "and we'll need to see well to do this right." Why risk bungling the task by working at night? Besides, they couldn't go anywhere right away even if their efforts succeeded. So Rus now lay sleepless, anxious for dawn to arrive.

Then, forcing themselves up despite their exhaustion, they set to work at sunrise. They punctured the jugs' plastic seals. They drained the water from the five full jugs they hadn't used. They brought the sixth jug. They carried all their supplies down to the riverbank yet again.

"This just might work," Jodie said, "but we'll have to make the jugs watertight if they're gonna float."

"What do you mean, watertight?" Matt asked.

"So they won't leak. They don't have caps, right? If we leave them open, the spouts will let water in. So the question is, how can we seal them?"

"Tape," Matt suggested.

"That might've worked," Rus noted, "if we hadn't used it up already."

Matt blurted, "Wooden plugs! You know, like corks. Only cut from wood."

Rus laughed at this suggestion. "That'd probably work," he admitted. "But all we have is scalpels, and

66

scalpels are such tiny knives they won't be good for carving wood. Six plugs would take a week. We need something quicker."

"Hey! Band aids!" Jodie shouted. "Matt suggested tape, but we're out of tape. We have lots of band aids, though."

Jodie and Matt exchanged glances. "It's worth a try," Matt said.

"*Band* aids?" Rus asked with a laugh.

Once they went ahead, Rus discovered that his doubt made sense. They used fifteen or twenty band aids to cap the spout on just one jug. They didn't stick very well on the plastic spout, and they were perforated, too, which let the water seep through. When the kids tested the jug in the river, the band aids leaked badly and soon fell off. "So much for band aids," Rus muttered.

They sat around, silent and gloomy, for several minutes. What else could they use to cap the spouts?

Looking at the medical supplies on the ground, Jodie exclaimed, "Gloves!"

Matt wrinkled his nose in dismay. "Gloves?"

"You know—surgical gloves."

Rus and Matt looked at each other. Matt said, "I don't get it."

Jodie leaned over, picked up the box of gloves, took out a packet, pulled it open, and removed one of the two gloves lying inside the paper envelope. It was an ordinary surgical glove: floppy, pale yellow rubber coated with fine white powder.

Rus said, "This is nuts."

"Just watch." Jodie grabbed the wrist opening, shoved it up against her mouth, and blew. The glove inflated slightly, forming a puffy hand. "Air-tight." Rus felt baffled by this odd demonstration. "I still don't get it."

"*I* do!" Matt exclaimed. "You'll put the glove over the jug's spout."

"Right," Jodie said. At once she forced the glove's wrist opening over the two-inch-wide spout. It went on tightly enough to seal the hole.

Rus felt uncertain. "Well. . ."

"It works, doesn't it?"

"It'll work," he said, "if it'll stay on." He reached out, grabbed the glove and pulled. It came right off. "See? No good."

Before she could speak, though, Matt said, "No problem. There's that tourniquet stuff, right? Those strips of yellow rubber that nurses put around your arm before they stick you for a blood sample. Let's use some of that."

"Around the glove?" Jodie asked.

"To hold it in place."

Putting it on turned out as simple as if they'd been using big rubber bands. Within a few minutes, they had all six water jugs securely capped.

But now they faced another task: attaching the jugs to the platform. This presented a more difficult problem than the platform itself. They were out of wire and tape. Vines might work, and they tried them, but vines didn't hold, either. For a while, the kids felt defeated. Then Jodie experimented with the tourniquet rubber and found that it worked almost like bungee cords to fasten the jugs onto the wooden platform. With great effort they strapped the jugs into place.

Soon the raft rested upside-down on the riverbank with the six plastic jugs attached—one at each corner and one at the midpoint on each of two sides. The kids stared at their handiwork for a long moment.

"Well, I guess we'd better test it," Matt said.

"Here we go again," Rus said, dreading what would happen next.

"Give it a try," Jodie said. "Flip it into the water."

18

Jodie took her place on the near side of the raft. Matt and Rus took their places, too. They all reached down.

"One, two, three—*lift!*" Rus shouted.

Even together they were too weak to raise the raft more than part way up.

"Let's try again," Jodie said. "One— Two— Three!"

At that moment all of them hoisted that side until the raft stood vertically, then toppled into the water, where it sat without moving.

Matt waded in and boosted himself onto the platform. It held his weight.

Then Jodie came over and hopped aboard. The raft held her weight, too, riding about six inches above the water. She felt a tingle of delight. "It's good!"

Matt reached out and shook her. "We did it!"

Standing on the riverbank, Rus looked unimpressed. "This had better work."

"Oh, come on," Jodie scolded, "it's great."

"Let's hope it hangs together."

"It'll work," Matt said. "We're on our way."

Then Jodie thought of something. They weren't quite ready yet. With so little equipment, why leave anything behind? "Wait—our stuff."

"What stuff?" Rus asked, sounding confused.

"Back at the plane," she said. "Our packs. The medical gear, too." Without speaking, Jodie hopped off, landed knee-deep in the water, then grabbed the raft's edge and towed it back to shore. "Let's get going," she said. "It's already late."

Together they ran to the crash site, gathered up anything that looked useful, and returned to the raft.

Rus helped them stow the gear—three small backpacks, two water bottles, two spare T-shirts, a roll of sheet plastic, and the medical supplies. The he boosted himself onto the platform.

Climbing back onto the raft again, Jodie felt a flutter of panic in her belly. She wanted to get away from the plane and the forest surrounding it, yet she worried about leaving. Where would they end up? Could they really reach one of the towns down river? Would they reach safety—or just get in even worse trouble? She couldn't believe she'd ever hesitate to leave this place, but she did.

"Wait a minute!" Matt blurted. "The pilots!"

Jodie saw Rus give Matt a peculiar look. "What about them?"

"Maybe we should, you know—" He faltered, then forced the words out: "—*bury* them."

Rus grabbed some of the supplies from Matt. "You've got to be kidding. We couldn't even pry them out of there if we tried."

"But don't you think—"

"Look, if we're gonna go, let's go. If we don't really hustle, we'll end up dead, too, just like them," Rus said. "Let's clear out."

Jodie crouched uncomfortably on the raft. Rus was right. There wasn't anything more they could do. It was time to leave.

Startling her, Matt hopped off, splashed back to shore, and grabbed three thick branches lying on the riverbank.

"What are *those*?" Jodie asked as he climbed aboard.

"Poles," he said. "To push with." He stuck one in the water and gave a shove. Jodie and Rus took the others and started pushing against the river bottom.

The raft eased into the current.

Part Three

The Raft

19

The raft worked. Rus couldn't quite believe it, but it worked. The network of saplings and branches held together, the tourniquet rubber kept the six empty water jugs in place, and the jugs made the whole thing float. The only problem wasn't even serious: finding somewhere comfortable to sit on the grid of branches. *So what,* Rus told himself. At least they were on their way. In a day or so they'd reach a town and leave this sweaty jungle.

The poles worked, too. When shoved against the river bottom, they turned out to be fairly useful for nudging the raft along. Rus hated to admit it, but Matt had come up with yet another good idea. So now he picked up one of the poles from where it lay on the platform, swung the pole around, and angled it into the water. He probed. Deeper than he thought—Rus couldn't even find the bottom. He pulled the pole up, then shoved it down again. "There!" Rus shouted, feeling the tip touch something. He probed again, shoving hard.

"Hey, that's good," Jodie said. "It really helped."

Rus lifted the pole, plunged it in, and pushed. The raft definitely went faster than before. Soon he got the hang of it and worked up a rhythm.

"Okay, guys, let's get out of here."

Sitting up front, Jodie watched the landscape changing. The raft eased around a bend in the river. Trees went by. The water widened, narrowed, widened yet again. Three butterflies orbited Jodie for a moment like fluttery planets, then veered off into space. Huge clouds billowed overhead. The light shifted on the water. The only sounds came from forest birds and from

73

the watery noise of Rus swishing his pole in and out of the river.

The rainforest troubled her. In many ways it looked much as Jodie had anticipated—lush and green and intricate—yet it was completely different. She had expected to find a gentle paradise, not a place that caused her new discomforts at every turn. The rainforest. She had never imagined that something so beautiful could be so scary, or that something so scary could be so beautiful.

Matt loved the raft. It didn't go fast, but at least it went, and he felt thrilled that his invention worked. Two points for Matt! Jodie looked pleased with the raft, too, and even Rus admitted it was pretty neat. Now all they had to do was ride down river, reach a town or city, and phone Dad at the clinic. Matt could hardly wait to see people's faces when the raft sailed into view. *Whoa, get a load of that!* they'd exclaim. Then someone would comment, *I bet that eight-year-old was the one who figured out such a cool invention.* And everyone would cheer as Matt led his sister and his cousin off the raft.

"How long d'you think it'll take us to reach that town?" he asked.

"Well," Rus said, poking his pole into the river, "that'll depend on how far away the town is, won't it?"

"I guess so."

"Assuming there *is* a town," Rus added.

Jodie, staring at the trees, perked up. "What do you mean, *assuming?*"

Rus huffed. "Just what I said. We're assuming there's a town nearby."

Matt resented Rus's doubts. "I told you I saw a town," he stated firmly.

"Yeah, you told us that," Rus said. "But did you really *see* a town?"

"Of course I did."

74

"Let me get this straight," Jodie interrupted. "Are you thinking maybe there's no town after all?"

Rus shoved hard with his pole; the raft grunted under his weight. "Oh, there's a town somewhere. Probably lots of towns. Question is, where? And how far down river? And on *which* river?"

"I saw it," Matt insisted. He started to feel angry that Rus didn't believe him.

"You saw *something*."

"Sort of a rough area that could've been houses," Matt said.

"*Could've* been?"

Annoyed, Matt shouted, "I saw it! I really did!"

Matt was relieved when Jodie stopped the argument. "Look, guys, let's don't hassle each other. Let's just go down river and reach that town, okay?"

"Fine!" Matt declared.

Rus stared at him without smiling. "Let's hope you really saw a town."

Matt turned away. With his back to Jodie and Rus, he tried to catch whatever they said, but they didn't speak.

Had that been a town he'd seen from the plane, Matt wondered suddenly—or just a reflection on the water? And was the town close enough that this weird little raft could reach it before they all collapsed from hunger?

Rus was surprised by how sore he felt. Poling the raft along shouldn't have been hard work—he just stuck the pole in, leaned on it, and eased the raft forward—but he soon felt achy and exhausted. His arms had been cramping from the start, and now his legs wouldn't stop trembling. At times Rus felt so dizzy that he almost lost his balance. He had always prided himself on his strength and stamina, but he soon felt weak, almost faint. What was happening?

Then at once he understood. He hadn't eaten a decent meal in three days; he hadn't eaten anything at all in almost forty-eight hours. His body was screaming at him for food. Head pounding, Rus sat down abruptly.

"You okay?" Jodie asked him.

"Just great," he replied, resting his forehead in his hands. He had saved one last candy bar—the Milky Way he'd hidden in his pack—and Rus couldn't imagine anything he'd rather do than eat it. Not a good move, though. One, he'd have to fend off Jodie and Matt. Two, this might not be the best time anyway. Save something for a bad day, he told himself. Things were tough, but they might get even tougher. Just in case, he'd save the Milky Way for later.

"Want some water?" Jodie held out her canteen.

He shook his head. "It's not water I need, it's a pepperoni pizza."

"Yeah!" Matt joined in. "Or chili dogs! That's it—chili dogs!"

Rus felt even more miserable as Matt and Jodie started jabbering about all the food they craved. He wished he'd never even joked about his hunger.

"—and lasagna!"

"Or baked ziti!"

"And some Chinese food, too!"

"And ice cream!"

"Right—double chocolate chunk!"

His head spun. For a moment, Rus thought he'd pass out. Only his fear of falling into the river pulled him back from the edge.

This was almost unbearable. Not just the physical discomforts. Not the bugs. Not the constant ache of hunger. It was something else. The helplessness. The sense of being too weak to solve the problems he faced. He wouldn't survive that long, Rus told himself, if he kept getting weaker and weaker.

20

Late that morning, after they'd docked the raft for a brief rest, Jodie looked around in the forest and tried to find something to eat. Didn't lots of fruit grow in the rainforest? There had to be something. Jodie couldn't imagine how she could keep on going otherwise. She felt especially concerned about Matt, who looked terrible—draggy, dazed, and blotchy with bug bites. How much longer could he hold out? She was determined to find her brother some food.

No such luck. Then, suddenly, she noticed something overhead. A peculiar dark green fruit grew ten or fifteen feet off the ground in a leafy tree. A coconut? No, too dark and long. One of those bad-tasting pods they'd found earlier? This looked much bigger. She didn't know what she'd spotted, but she decided to check it out. Gazing upward, she felt confident of her ability to shimmy high enough to have a look.

She grabbed hold of the trunk and pulled herself up. She raised her hands higher on the trunk. Boosted her legs up. Raised her hands again. And in this way, like a caterpillar inching up a twig, Jodie worked her way higher.

She reached the green thing within a few minutes. What was it? She couldn't see it well in the midst of so much shadowy vegetation. Jodie tried to remember the rainforest fruits. Mango, papaya, guava: just a few names came to mind. Jodie stared for a few seconds at the thing dangling in front of her. Then, sweating hard, she let go with her left hand, reached out, and snatched it right off the tree. She dropped it and grabbed for the tree again, desperately, to avoid falling.

Jodie struggled to descend but reached the ground without any mishaps. "Matt!" she called out. "Rus!"

77

One of the boys shouted back.

She picked the fruit up from the forest floor. "Look what I found!" she hollered, heading back to where Matt and Rus waited near the raft.

"What the heck is *that*?" Matt asked when his sister rushed over with a weird-looking fruit. It was the size and shape of a football but covered with bumps.

"I don't know," Jodie said. "I pulled it off a tree."

"Give it to me," Rus ordered, snatching it from Jodie's grip.

"It's mine!" She grabbed it back.

Watching them struggle, Matt worried they'd tear the thing to bits, whatever it was, ruining their chances for a meal. He felt so hungry that even the possibility of food made him shake.

"Just 'cause you found it doesn't mean it's yours!" Rus shouted.

Matt dashed over to the raft, poked around in the boxes of medical gear, found a scalpel, and raced back to Rus and Jodie. "You guys are a bunch of jerks," he told them. "Why don't you figure out if it's really worth fighting over?"

His sister and his cousin fell silent. Staring at him, Jodie said, "Well—"

"Here," Rus said. He took the scalpel. With a couple of strokes he sliced the fruit in half.

Matt stared at what lay in Rus's hands.

Inside a thick skin was some creamy white stuff with big black seeds embedded there.

"Is it rotten?" Matt asked.

"Seems okay," Rus said, sniffing one of the pieces.

Jodie took the other piece and sniffed it, too. "Smells like yogurt." She poked her finger into the stuff and licked it cautiously. "Tastes like yogurt!" Suddenly she shoved her face against the fruit and started gobbling.

78

Rus immediately started devouring the other piece.

Matt felt helpless watching them eat. Would there be any left for him?

Then Jodie stopped herself and held out the piece of fruit. "Here." White stuff covered her lips and cheeks.

Carefully at first, Matt took a nibble. He couldn't decide what the fruit tasted like. He didn't care. He knew only that it was so sweet, rich, pure, and good that a shiver went up his spine and tears came to his eyes.

Rus followed Jodie back into the forest. If they could only find more of that fruit, the delay in leaving would be worthwhile. They'd boost their energy. They'd increase their chances of survival. But where, he wondered, was the right tree?

"This one," Jodie announced, stopping.

"You're sure."

"I guess so."

"You *guess* so."

"I don't see any fruit," Matt said, looking around.

They could have been anywhere in the rainforest. So little light penetrated the upper canopy that the time could have been twilight instead of noon. Craning his neck, Rus tried to spot more of the pods—what Matt had nicknamed football fruit—overhead. No such luck. He saw vines, flowers, branches, and a zillion leaves, but nothing that resembled what they'd eaten. "Must be the wrong place," Rus grumbled.

"It's the *right* place," Jodie insisted. "I'm sure of it."

"Then where's the fruit?"

"Heck if I know."

"Great."

"And besides, I never saw more than one of them anyway."

"There's got to be more," Matt stated. "It's a big jungle."

Rus felt more and more exasperated by this pointless search. "Come on—we can't look forever. We'll starve to death wandering around like this."

Jodie scanned the canopy. "So what are we supposed to do?"

"We'll go back to the raft," Rus said, "and head down river."

"But I'm hungry!" Matt whined.

Rus couldn't stay patient any longer. "Let's go. Maybe we'll find more football fruits somewhere else. Now we know there's at least *one* thing here that's edible, right?"

21

They set off again, drifting, not going fast but at least going, silent except for a few stutters and creaks when the kids moved around on the raft. Mostly they kept still. The fruit they'd eaten lingered like something imagined, not tasted—a flavor recalled from a dream. Matt hadn't gained much energy. If anything, that creamy sweet stuff reminded him how little he'd eaten. He could fill his belly with water, but nothing took away his hunger. Matt couldn't believe how weak he felt. All he wanted to do was lie down, doze off, and let the river carry him away.

Matt had nearly fallen asleep when he heard Rus ask, "Is this place, you know, inhabited?"

At once he felt wide awake. It wasn't Rus's question that startled him—it was the touch of fear in his voice. *Inhabited.* As if that somehow made things worse, not better. Matt looked over at his sister. Jodie had read a lot of books about the rainforest and would know the answer.

"Of course it's inhabited," she snapped. "What do you suppose Dad and the doctors are doing operations on—toucans?"

For a moment, Matt expected Rus to lash out at her—he'd taunt her, hassle her, even give her a shove—but he didn't. He didn't even stare his death-ray stare. He just sat there, serious and silent, watching her. Which startled Matt still more. Rus would have to be pretty worried to pass up hassling Jodie.

"So who lives here, anyway?" Rus asked.

Matt waited for the speech he knew would follow. Given half a chance, Jodie would rattle on all day long about the rainforest.

Yet now she spoke only one word: "Indians."

"Of course they're Indians," Rus noted. "But what *kind* of Indians?"

Jodie shrugged. "Lots of different tribes. Ocama. Iquito. Yagua—"

"No," Rus said. "That's not what I mean."

Matt couldn't restrain himself any longer. They weren't getting to the point. "What Rus means," he interrupted, "is—are they *safe.*"

Rus shrugged. "Well, yeah. I guess that's it."

"Safe?" Jodie asked.

"Safe to be around," Matt added.

Jodie started to speak, but Rus interrupted her. "I read this book at school. *In the Darkest Jungle,* or something like that. This guy goes to Ecuador to set up a school in an Indian village. He hikes and hikes through the forest and nearly drops dead from exhaustion. Then some Indians find him and take him to their village."

"What *I* think," Jodie said, "is that the Indians will *rescue* us—"

"Let me finish. The guy in the book thinks he's been rescued, too. But once he reaches the village, he sees this rack with little heads hanging by their hair—"

"That's not true!" Jodie yelled.

"It said so in the book," Rus stated.

"Well, the author got it wrong," she said. "Or maybe the book was old. Some tribes used to shrink their enemies' heads a long time ago."

"Oh? How long?"

Matt felt more and more uneasy. Shrunken heads!

"Years ago," Jodie said with a casual gesture. "Ten, twenty, thirty years."

"You're sure?" Rus asked.

"Positive. Dad told me."

"Well, *that's* reassuring! He said we'd be safe flying to the clinic, too, so don't tell me Jack's so reassuring—"

"Stop it!" Matt shouted, feeling more and more agitated.

Rus and Jodie turned to him at once.

"You're just wasting your time," he told them. "Both of you."

A stuttering sound caught Matt's attention: a loud noise from a cluster of trees the raft was passing just then. All three kids turned, startled, listening hard. Matt couldn't see any creature that might have made that noise. Maybe Indians. . . ?

Matt said, "It's not just whether the Indians shrink heads or not. Maybe they don't. What I'm wondering is—are they friendly at all?"

"Of course they are," Jodie reassured him. "Remember Dad's great stories? The people who come to the mission? How kind and gentle they are?"

"We're not at the mission," Rus said. "We're in the middle of nowhere. And one of the doctors said there's still undiscovered tribes."

"The word's *uncontacted*," Jodie told Rus.

"Whatever."

"Uncontacted doesn't mean they're hostile."

"No," Rus replied, "but it means we'd better be careful."

Jodie shook her head. "Everything I've heard about rainforest people tells me they're okay."

Matt wondered if that was really true.

"They're nice," Jodie said.

"Oh, come on!" Rus exclaimed.

"It's true!" Jodie shouted. "They're not savages."

"I didn't say they're savages."

"They're a whole lot nicer than *you*, anyway."

Matt braced himself for Rus's counterattack. He'd blast her with angry words. He'd mock her till Jodie struck back. He might even punch her.

"I have a question," Rus said abruptly. "When are you gonna come to your senses? The world isn't a church picnic. There's some really bad people out there, and even the ones that aren't bad still look out only for themselves."

"Just like you."

He chuckled. "Of course. Life means survival of the fittest. Who else is gonna help you but yourself?"

"Other people," Jodie said.

"Ha!"

"Lots of people—people you don't even know."

"I'm not taking the risk," Rus said. He used his pole to push the raft away from the riverbank. "Especially in a place where Indians hunt people, kill them, shrink their heads, and hang 'em up on a rack."

Matt felt so troubled by these words that he couldn't even speak.

It almost seemed that Rus had been reading her mind, Jodie thought. She didn't share his hostile attitude toward the Indians, but she'd been wondering about the situation, too. Was it possible that people actually lived here? That seemed likely. Still, she hadn't seen anyone. Did that mean that no one was nearby? Or that Indians observed them, hidden, from within the forest?

The idea of someone silently watching her made Jodie tense with alarm. What would account for such sneakiness? Maybe the Indians feared them.

Or was fear what the *Coopers* should have been feeling. . . ?

Jodie could recall a few worrisome stories. The tribes in some areas remained almost entirely isolated, having succeeded in keeping outsiders out of their territory. Dad had mentioned several incidents in which Indians armed with spears and war clubs had attacked missionaries, prospectors, or Peruvian government officials. Hardly surprising, Dad said: some of these outsiders were attempting to steal the Indians' land. There had been some bad situations—lots of injuries and a few deaths. Even United Medical's doctors and support staff had been warned to stay clear of those areas.

Which areas? Jodie couldn't remember. Somewhere up near the border with Ecuador. Not far from the clinic where Dad worked, but farther west.

Jodie glanced at her brother and her cousin. Frightened by her own thoughts, she wanted to speak with them about what concerned her. She'd get it out of her head. Rus and Matt would calm her. Everything would be fine.

Or would it? What if the Badger had crashed in one of those isolated tribes' terrain? Would the Indians view three American kids as innocent arrivals worthy of compassion and help?

Or would they see them as trespassers deserving only fear, anger, and hostility?

Jodie stared at the forest surrounding her. A tan, hook-beaked bird—some kind of hawk—watched her warily from its roost on a dead tree. Otherwise she saw no other creature.

Either we're totally alone here, Jodie told herself, *or we're not.*

She couldn't decide which possibility was more terrifying.

22

Somewhat later—Matt couldn't even guess when—he roused from a nap and looked around. Jodie lay crumpled beside him. Rus slouched at the back of the raft. No one moved or spoke. Trees went by.

Looking at his right arm, Matt noticed a red tinge on his normally pale skin. His thighs, too, looked bright pink. Both legs, both arms, and the back of his neck felt prickly and tender. "Hey," Matt blurted, "we're getting sunburned!"

Rus turned to gaze at him. "Maybe *you* are."

"You are, too." Rus was even lighter-skinned than Jodie or Matt, and his neck and arms looked reddish orange. "You're a regular ol' lobster!"

Rus turned away in disgust. "Who cares."

Jodie forced herself up. "What's going on?"

Matt felt alarmed when he saw how awful she looked—face puffy, eyes bloodshot, arms and legs deep pink. "Sunburn," he said.

Jodie sat up suddenly. Glancing at her thighs and arms, she spoke in a low voice that worried Matt even more than if she'd shouted. "Hey, this isn't good."

"It's October," Rus stated firmly. "You don't get sunburned in October."

"You do when you're this close to the Equator," Jodie told him. "The sun is blasting away, and these clothes don't protect us much."

"There's nothing we can do about it," Rus said.

Matt felt more and more concerned. He didn't want to get zapped by the sun. "Are we gonna be okay?" he asked his sister.

"Not if we don't protect ourselves," she stated. "We're already feeling crummy. How are we gonna feel when we're half-cooked, too?"

Rus shrugged. "Medium rare."

"It's not a joke," she told him.

"What's the big deal if we get a tan?" Rus asked.

"We're not talking about a tan, bozo. We're talking about a burn. People can get sick from sunburn. *Real* sick. Especially if you're already in bad shape."

"Speak for yourself."

"You don't look so hot, either."

Matt said, "This is worse than last year at the beach."

"Don't waste my time," Rus grumbled.

Jodie threw her hands up in disgust. "Look, you know this is a problem. Let's do something about it."

Rus shrugged again. "Not my department. Ask the professor."

Matt squirmed when he saw both Rus and Jodie staring at him. He felt more and more uncomfortable. "Well—"

"We're waiting," Rus announced.

"Give him a chance!" Jodie scolded.

The truth was, Matt couldn't think of a single good idea. He tried and tried, but his brain wasn't working right. He felt too hot, too sore, too hungry. His inability to solve this problem terrified him. How could they deal with the difficulties facing them, he wondered, if he couldn't even think straight?

"When you figure it out," Rus told Matt, "send me an e-mail."

I can't stand him, Jodie told herself. *He's the worst person in the world.* She couldn't imagine how she'd tolerate her cousin's presence any longer. She'd shove him off the raft. Better yet, she'd jump off, swim to shore, and set off on foot. Anything would be easier than putting up with Rus Cooper. Even dying in the rainforest would be better than being with him. . .

Well, that was taking things too far. Besides, Matt needed her. But how, she wondered, would she endure Rus's company?

Fuming, Jodie watched some long-legged bugs skating on the water.

Something caught her attention: a buzzing noise.

The bugs? No, too loud. And different.

"Hey!" Jodie hollered suddenly. She fell silent, listening hard.

Rus and Matt stared at her, then suddenly started looking all around.

"A rescue plane!" Matt shouted.

"*Some* kind of plane." She couldn't identify the source of the noise. It didn't seem to grow loud or soft; it just went on and on, neither close nor distant.

"Hey!" Matt started yelling. "Over here!"

Rus shoved him. "It's too far off. They'll never hear you."

"So what do we do?"

"Just hope it flies closer, then start waving like maniacs."

"At least we're out in the open now," Jodie reassured herself. An image came to her: a pontoon-equipped plane circling, then landing right on the river.

"Hey!" Matt hollered. "Down here!" He started waving wildly.

"Stop it," Rus said.

"I won't!"

"The sound's already fading."

Jodie listened. When she realized that Rus was right—the buzzing faded more with each passing second—a great wave of despair washed through her. She could barely keep from crying.

Rus glanced at her, then away. "At least they haven't given up."

* * *

Matt couldn't believe that the rescue plane hadn't found them. It hadn't even come close enough for them to see it. For a long time after he'd heard the airplane's noise, Matt waited and waited, staring at the sky.

He stared so hard that he didn't even notice the changes right overhead. He came to his senses only when he felt rain soaking him. The downpour started so suddenly that it was like someone up there flicked a switch. "Whoa!" Matt called out.

"Just what we need," Rus grumbled.

The staticky noise grew deafening. The river turned rough from all the raindrops striking it. Within minutes Matt started shivering. He and Jodie huddled together, hugging their legs and pressing their faces against their knees.

How was it possible, Matt wondered, that he could feel any worse than he already felt? Yet now he did. He began to shake uncontrollably.

"—raincoats!" Jodie shouted.

"What?" Matt asked. He could barely hear past the rain's racket.

"If only we'd brought our raincoats!"

Rus shot them an angry glance. "For starters."

Matt hunched forward, chilled and achy, and wished he were anywhere else on earth.

23

The rain stopped; the clouds broke up; pink light shifted on the river. Rus wondered if they should find a place to camp overnight.

Suddenly a fish leaped, flashed in the sunlight, and hit the water.

Jodie, watching, said, "Nice."

Just like Jodie, Rus thought. *As if we're on a nature trip!*

Another fish broke the surface, sending out ripples.

"Did you see that?" Jodie asked, loudly now.

"Who cares?" Rus muttered.

"But that's it!" Jodie exclaimed. "That's what we'll eat."

"Fish!" Matt yelled.

Rus laughed harshly. "Sure, I'll just pull out my rod and start casting." What a laugh—as if the fish would leap into their hands!

"I didn't say it'll be simple," Jodie said, "but there must be *some* way."

Rus sat back, leaning on his elbows. "Yeah, right."

Jodie and Matt started rummaging through the supply boxes.

"I know!" Matt shouted. "Plastic!"

"Plastic?" Rus asked in annoyance.

"Yeah—we could sort of scoop the fish up in a sheet of plastic."

Even Jodie laughed at him. "Sorry, Matt. No go on *that* idea."

They returned to poking around in the box. Jodie pulled out a tangle of wire they'd salvaged from the plane. "How about this?" she asked. "It's thicker than fishing line but strong. We could bend the end to make a fish hook."

Rus's first thought was to make fun of her, but he held off. He felt so hungry that the idea of fishing started to intrigue him. Maybe they could work it out. Jodie's idea wasn't as dumb as when Matt suggested plastic. "Copper wire's too soft," he told her. "Even a dinky fish could bend it and escape."

"But maybe—"

"And the wire's thick enough that fish would see it and shy away."

"Can't we just *try* it?" Jodie whined.

"All right!" Rus shouted. "Let's waste half the afternoon on a hopeless idea!" Furious, he reached over to the tangle of wire. Getting a length of it loose wasn't difficult; the hard part was removing the insulation. Rus peeled some free with a scalpel blade, then stripped the rest with his fingers. Fifteen minutes' work produced about a yard of bare wire.

Wire, he thought. *For fishing.* Rus bent the end of the wire to form a crude fishhook. As if a fish would waste its time biting a piece of wire. There wasn't even any bait! "All right," Rus said. "Satisfied?"

Jodie smiled her cheeriest smile. "Well, it *might* work."

At least half an hour passed. No fish bit. They didn't so much as jiggle the line. Increasingly impatient, Rus wanted to yank the wire out, wad it up, and toss it away. He held off: at least this experiment had silenced Matt and Jodie.

Or had it?

Rus turned to Matt, who was rummaging through the medical supplies.

"So we need some kind of string," Matt said.

"Line," Rus corrected.

"Line, whatever." He sat back on his heels.

Matt's solemn expression started to annoy Rus. He took himself so seriously! But since he might be onto something, Rus kept quiet.

"Suture is line, right?" Matt said abruptly. "Just like fishing line."

"What are you thinking?" Jodie asked.

"Suture. You know—surgical thread for stitching wounds." He plunged his hands into one of the boxes, rummaged there briefly, and pulled out a little packet. Blue on one side, silver on the other. There was writing on the blue side that Rus couldn't see clearly. Matt shouted, "This!"

"I don't get it," Rus told him.

Matt pulled open the packet. Inside was a coil of black thread. "Fishing line!"

Interesting—but Rus saw at once that his idea wouldn't work. "Same problem as the wire," he said. "It's too thick and too short. The fish will see it."

"Fine!" Matt shouted. But instead of acting annoyed, he got more and more excited. "There's different kinds. I've seen Dad stock the supply cabinets at work. There's dark stuff, light stuff—" He rummaged through the contents of the box again, pulling out several packets. "There's even clear stuff."

"Clear?"

"Like, you know, fishing line."

Rus started to wonder. If they could really find some clear line. . .

"Here," Matt said, holding out another packet. He ripped it open.

Inside was a coil of pale yellow filament. It wasn't really clear, but Rus saw that it was light enough to resemble eight- or ten-pound fishing line.

"That's it!" Jodie shouted. "That's really it!"

Rus felt a surge of excitement, then immediate disappointment. "Sorry, folks—no go. We still need a decent fish hook."

"But look here," Jodie said. She dangled something from the suture. Shaped like one third of a small circle, it was shiny steel. "The needle. Doctors use these things to stitch up cuts."

"It's not really a hook, though," Rus noted, but he understood a moment later why this didn't matter.

"It would be if it's *bent*," Jodie told him.

"Well—I guess so." Without saying more, Rus took one end of the curved needle in each hand, inhaled deeply, and tried to bend it. "Uh!" he exclaimed, then held out the needle for everyone to see.

It looked the same as before.

"Shoot!" he exclaimed. "It's impossible."

"Try again," Jodie said.

Rus shoved it at her. *You* try."

Jodie took the needle, grasped it carefully, and struggled to bend it. She made no progress. "It's stainless steel," Jodie said. "Tough stuff."

Matt tried, too, and also failed.

"No tools," Jodie said. "That's our problem."

"Brilliant insight," Rus told her.

"We need some pliers."

"Pliers?" Rus asked.

Jodie rummaged through the boxes of medical supplies. "There's a kind of surgical pliers I've seen Dad prepare for the doctors," she said. She poked around in the box. "None here, though."

"So much for that," Matt said.

They drifted for several minutes. A bird called out from a nearby tree: *Are you. . . fine?*

Rus felt more and more discouraged. How many more setbacks could they tolerate?

24

Jodie watched Rus groggily.

He was rummaging around in the boxes of medical supplies. Pulling out a packet of sutures, he opened it, unwound the pale thread, and let the needle dangle. He stared at it.

"What are you doing?" Jodie asked him.

He didn't answer. He simply put the needle in his mouth—tucked it between his upper and lower teeth—and bit down hard.

"You'll hurt yourself!"

Rus struggled for a moment, grimacing, as he shoved his thumb against the needle. Then he removed it from his mouth. Instead of a curve, the needle's shape now resembled a V.

"There's our fishhook," Rus announced.

Suddenly wide awake, Jodie stared at the suture needle in his hand. It really did look like a fishhook. Would it work like one, too? It had no barbs to catch on a fish's mouth. Maybe that wouldn't matter. . . Or maybe an improvised hook wouldn't be good enough. All she knew was that Rus had come closer to making the real thing than she would ever have thought possible. "You did it!" she cried.

When he grinned, Jodie saw a smear of red on his teeth.

"Rus, you're bleeding."

He rubbed his right index finger across his mouth, then looked at the blood on his hand. He rubbed it on his shorts. "So?"

"So let's go fishing!" Matt shouted.

Rus's smile faded. "Sorry to disappoint you, pal," he said, "but the fishies don't bite just because we offer them a hook."

"We need bait?" Matt asked.

"That's how it usually works."

Jodie felt her spirits sink: yet another problem to solve.

The raft kept drifting.

"What do fish eat, anyway?" she asked.

"It depends on the fish," Rus said. "Mostly bugs or other fish."

"We could catch some bugs," Matt suggested.

"Maybe. That might take a long time, though."

Jodie fought a growing sense of despair. She felt so hungry that her whole body ached—joints throbbed, head pounded, hands trembled. The river teemed with fish, yet they swam beyond her grasp! Having invented this fishing gear made the situation even more painful than if they'd never succeeded.

Rus said, "Get me a scalpel."

"Why a scalpel?"

"Just get me one."

Jodie couldn't imagine what he was thinking. Reaching back to the supply box, however, she found one of the handles and a foil packet with a curved blade pictured on the front. She handed both to Rus.

He took the handle and set it on his lap. Then, ripping open the packet, he removed the blade, grabbed the handle, and snapped the blade into place.

"What are you doing?" Jodie asked.

Rus held the scalpel thoughtfully in his right hand. Then, without hesitating, he reached out to his left arm, stared for a moment at the cuts there, brought the scalpel blade down to one particular cut—one with a small flap of skin that dangled from Rus's arm—and sliced off the flap. Then he picked up the flap, neatly snagged it onto the improvised fishhook, and, holding the line in his left hand, tossed the hook overboard.

"Eeew!" Matt squealed.

Jodie couldn't even react. Something silenced her just then: realizing how much Rus had suffered. She had always thought of her cousin as peculiar. Peculiar and, at the same time, sad in a way that made Rus seem distant even when he stood right next to her. Some sort of wall or shell enclosed him. Looking just like Rus, this shell protected him yet encased him—shut him inside something hard. That was what made him peculiar, she realized: his hardness. And somehow Jodie now saw that hardness more clearly than she ever had before.

How hard did you have to be, really, to use your own flesh as fishing bait?

Matt watched Rus fishing with the gear that they'd invented. Breaking off a skinny branch from one of the saplings that made up the raft's platform, Rus had tied several lengths of suture, end to end, onto the branch. Then he had dangled the suture needle into the water. It was a neat invention. So neat, Matt told himself, that *he* should have invented it!

Too tired to argue, Matt fell silent. Maybe Rus was right. They hadn't eaten for so long that Matt couldn't even remember when he'd had his last meal. He wasn't crazy about fish—the only kind he liked was filet sandwiches at McDonald's—but maybe he'd try it after all.

"Can't I take a turn?" he asked softly.

Rus shoved the branch at him. "So do it! Just don't drop it in the water."

Matt took the pole, held it carefully, and watched the line shift closer to him. What was going on beneath the surface? He imagined swarms of fish down there, checking out the hook and deciding whether to bite or not. Were they the kind that McDonald's put in fish sandwiches?

The line jerked. Startled, Matt nearly lost his grip on the pole.

"Keep hold of it!" Rus shouted. "Don't let go!"

Then, with a single yank, a fish flew out of the water and landed on the raft. It flopped about making a funny noise, not slap-slap-slap but a fluttery sound like pigeons taking off.

"I've got one!" Matt hollered.

They all just stared. Only five or six inches long, the fish was nearly flat, silver on the upper half and blood-red on the lower.

Rus reached down to grab it.

"Don't!" Jodie shouted suddenly. "It's a piranha!"

As she spoke, Matt saw the teeth—pointy teeth that snapped again and again as the fish flipped around on the raft's plastic floor—and the harder Matt tried to escape the closer it came. "No!" he screamed, backing off. "Keep it away from me!"

There was no place to go. Matt lost his balance, but Jodie caught him by the arm just as he tipped toward the water. Then he flung his right arm backwards to keep his balance, which tugged the pole and the line, and the fish leaped closer, striking Matt's right foot.

"No!"

The piranha would bite him. The white teeth would sink into his flesh. The jaws would gobble chunks from his leg. Panicking, Matt would topple into the river, where a swarm of piranhas would set to work eating him alive. Within minutes only a tattered skeleton would remain.

"Relax," Rus said wearily. He reached out to the fishing line, grabbed it, and pulled it closer. He dangled the fish about a foot above the raft's floor. Helpless, it snapped repeatedly at the line but stayed far enough from everyone to be harmless.

Matt stared in amazement and fear. He'd never seen such a scary creature in his life. He couldn't believe that Rus could hold it so calmly. It would gobble up the fishing line, work its way to Rus's fingers, and start in on *him!*

"What are you going to do!" Jodie shrieked.

"Nothing," Rus answered with a faint smile. "Time is on my side."

The fish took five minutes to die. The jaws opened and closed more slowly; the flopping eased, then stopped. Soon the fish dangled, limp, on the line. Matt felt relieved at first, then frightened. What if the fish was faking—just waiting till someone reached out to touch it?

"*Now* what do we do?" Jodie asked.

Matt saw Rus's face show annoyance and surprise. "What do we *do?*"

"Well, *you* know." She gestured uncomfortably at the fish.

"After three whole days without food," Rus said, "you're not sure?"

"But it's raw!" Matt exclaimed.

"Of course it's raw."

A look of disgust came over Jodie's face. "You'll eat it just like that?"

Rus shoved the shiny fish at her like a knife. "Look, I'd cook it if I could. I'd build a campfire right there on the riverbank. I'd fry it with butter and sprinkle it with herbs. But we don't have a frying pan, do we? We don't even have any matches. So let's stop kidding ourselves and just eat it."

Matt squinched up his face. "Yuck!"

Laughing, Rus said, "It's no more disgusting than sushi."

"Who?" Matt asked.

"Sushi," Jodie told him. "That fancy raw fish that Mom and Dad eat at Japanese restaurants."

"You got it," Rus said. "This is sushi, too. Rainforest sushi."

"No way," Matt said. He started to gag.

Rus poked around in the medical box. He pulled out a paper packet, removed a scalpel blade, and snapped it onto one of the handles. At once he set to work: slicing open the fish's belly and pulling out squiggly guts.

Matt thought he'd throw up.

Jodie turned pale. "Count me out."

Rus pulled out a tangle of insides and tossed them overboard. Then he said, "Boy, that was dumb—we could've used it for bait. Or even eaten it."

"*Stop!*" Jodie exclaimed.

Slashing at the fish's shiny skin, Rus didn't even look up. "You guys are so spoiled," he said. "What do you expect—some Indians will paddle up and serve you dinner on a silver tray? Get real." He peeled off a thin sheet of fish and held it out to her. It was pale, almost transparent. "This is what we've got."

Matt turned away, then looked back again. Would Rus really *eat* the stuff?

Rus shrugged. He looked at the piece of fish, then suddenly popped it into his mouth. He chewed and swallowed.

Jodie turned away. "Oh, *gross!*"

Matt squeezed his eyes shut when he saw Rus chewing. He couldn't believe he'd actually done that. Then again, he *could* believe it. Rus would do anything. Within a few minutes, he'd eaten most of the fish. Matt couldn't imagine taking even a single bite. If only they had a fire. . . If only they had a hamburger bun and some of that white fish sauce. . .

His stomach started cramping so hard he could hardly sit upright.

He wouldn't die of thirst or starvation, Rus decided that afternoon. He might not have anything good to drink, but at least he'd have water. He might not have much to eat, but at least he'd have fish. *Enough to keep*

99

body and soul together, as Mom used to say. That was all he really needed.

So Rus kept fishing. He opened more suture sets. He tied more lengths of surgical thread onto sticks. He dangled more lines into the water. He caught more fish. Not many—maybe one per hour—but enough. Enough to take the edge off his hunger. Enough to believe that hunger wasn't his biggest problem.

Jodie and Matt, though... Neither kid would even try the rainforest sushi. Dumb—how picky could they get? Granted, raw fish wasn't exactly a burger and fries, but they didn't have any choice right now. Rus couldn't believe that these two would pass up real food for the *idea* of food they'd rather have.

But that wasn't his problem. What difference did it make to him if they ate or not? In some ways it helped Rus if they didn't: all the more fish for him!

Survival of the fittest, right?

Sink or swim.

25

As the light faded and the kids looked around for a good place to beach the raft, Jodie wondered how far they'd gone that day. She couldn't even guess. Ten miles? Twenty? Not far enough, anyway: she saw no sign of a town or a village.

At least the raft was holding up, Jodie told herself. She felt as vulnerable as a spider floating downstream on a leaf, yet the raft was their haven—a little speck of safety in a treacherous world. They'd be fine now that they had the raft.

Poling it toward the riverbank, Jodie jumped off, grabbed the platform, and pulled it toward the muddy shore. Rus got off, too, and splashed through the water. She tensed up at the sight of all those scratches on his arms. It wasn't just the ugliness of his wounds that bothered her; she felt concerned about the pain he must have been feeling. He'd experienced so many hardships in just thirteen years, and now all this new discomfort. An alarming thought occurred to her: *They don't bite unless you're already wounded* Jodie couldn't imagine how uncomfortable Rus would feel with piranha bites, too. Luckily the fish didn't attack.

"I don't like how those cuts look," she said as they carried the boxes of medical supplies to the place they'd chosen as a campsite.

"What's it to you?" Rus asked. He sounded indifferent, yet she knew he felt concerned that she'd noticed, too. Were the cuts getting infected? They looked puffy and damp.

"Well—I'm, like, worried."

"Mind your own business."

Jodie gestured in annoyance. "We have to look after each other—"

"No we don't."

"We do. We really do."

"Look," Rus said. "I don't need you mothering me. I already had a mother and she didn't work out too great." Dumping his load of equipment, Rus walked back to the riverbank. Jodie let him avoid her; watching him at a distance, though, she lingered. She walked part way to where he stood but held off.

Pink-orange light twisted on the water, then faded to gray. Clouds of mosquitoes billowed in the air. Rus gazed across the river.

Jodie wanted to say something but didn't know what. She wanted to help Rus but didn't know how. Remembering how he'd cut himself on purpose to catch a fish, she wondered what she might ever do to make a difference to him. He seemed so alone. Jodie couldn't imagine how to help someone as strange and difficult as her cousin.

"Rus—"

He turned calmly, as if aware of her all along. "Beddy-bye time," Rus said, and he walked past her into the forest.

26

Nightfall came quickly. One moment the world was full of light, with a great molten mass of pink clouds overhead; a few minutes later, everything looked grainy with dusk.

Rus worried about being in the forest. On the water they could at least keep an eye on things. Among the trees he couldn't see more than five or ten yards even by day, and by night visibility dropped to one or two feet. How could he stay safe here, given the risks? How could he protect himself? It wasn't wild animals that worried him. What Rus feared were the larger, two-legged creatures—the kind with weapons far more dangerous than stingers.

But a tree that Rus had noticed in the forest—a huge tree with wall-like triangles of trunk extending from the main structure—suddenly gave him an idea. Where two of those wall-like pieces slanted off the trunk close together, they formed a compartment or cubicle that offered at least a little protection. Rus settled into one of those compartments with his back to the trunk and felt almost cozy.

"Where are you?" Jodie asked from somewhere close by in the dark.

"Right here," Rus said, "relaxing in the hot tub."

Even if they managed to avoid getting attacked, how long could they continue like this? Rus pondered the question but found no answer. They were in bad shape—weak, sore, and dazed from hunger. Matt, especially, seemed close to collapse. So many bug bites covered their skin that they looked bruised and lumpy, speckled with scabs. The cuts on Rus's left arm had grown puffy and incredibly sore. To his amazement, Jodie was okay—exhausted and irritable but pretty solid otherwise. Still, Rus couldn't feel confident that his cousins would maintain their stamina. He resented their presence. It was hard enough to save his own skin; it was far worse to have to think about his cousins, too. Rus was tired of having other people lean on him. He'd had plenty of that with Mom, he told himself, and look how things had turned out.

Rus couldn't help thinking about the last time he'd spoken with her. He had flown from New Jersey back to Iowa and had gone to the hospital where some doctors had been trying for several weeks to treat Mom's liver problems. "Fifth floor, room 519," someone had told him at the information desk. He'd bought her a candy bar at the gift shop—a Milky Way—and he took the elevator to the ward. Once he'd located the room, though, he found someone else there: a pot-bellied woman with a hideous tan, the kind you can fake by using cheap tinted suntan oil. "Sorry," he said on stepping into the woman's room, and he backed out at once.

"Rusty," a voice said as he retreated.

"Mom?" He stepped back into the room.

He couldn't believe this was his mother. Her skin was yellow-orange. Her tongue, when he glimpsed it, had a yellowish coating. Even her eyes were yellow. Her abdomen had swollen so much that she looked pregnant.

"How's it going?" Mom asked.

"Okay," Rus replied.

"Jack and Penny treating you fine?"

"Sure." He'd been living with his uncle, aunt, and cousins for months. They had welcomed Rus warmly, and their house was comfortable. Yet he resented them even worse than all the foster parents, since their cushy life reminded him that Mom's wasn't. She was in the hospital. She was dying.

"How's it going?" Rus asked.

104

"I don't feel too great." She gestured vaguely, both palms out. When she exhaled, Rus heard a gurgling sound. Mom soon noticed that Rus could hear this creepy noise. "Fluid in the lungs," she said calmly, like someone commenting on the weather.

"What do the doctors say?" Rus asked.

She smiled weakly. "I'm drowning."

"Drowning?"

"Drowning from the inside out."

He felt totally helpless. "Isn't there something I could, you know, *do?*"

She lifted a hand to her face. She placed it there for a second, pressing the cheek as if making sure that her flesh was still warm. Then she suddenly shoved the hand upward, running the fingers through her waxy hair. In a single breath she said, "Well thanks Sweetie but I don't know what that would be."

Rus didn't know how to respond, so he said, "I brought you something." He pulled the Milky Way from his pocket and held it out.

"Oh," Mom said. She took the candy. "That's real nice."

Later, after Mom had died, the hospital had given Rus a bag filled with her clothes and other belongings. One of the few things in the bag was that Milky Way. Rus had wondered ever since if Mom hadn't eaten it because she couldn't—maybe her stomach wouldn't tolerate that kind of food—or because she didn't like his gift.

Sitting there in the dark forest, Rus thought about eating his secret candy bar. It would be wonderful to have it now, he told himself. Milky Way. He was so hungry he couldn't imagine *not* eating it. Still, he decided to wait. He might need it when things got really rough.

You never knew when you might need a Milky Way.

27

How long had they been lost? Jodie lay awake all night tracking the time. They'd flown into Iquitos on Saturday morning; then they'd flown out and crashed that same afternoon. They'd stayed by the river Sunday, Monday, and early Tuesday. Then they'd set out on the raft. They had drifted all day Tuesday. Now it was Tuesday night.

No, Jodie told herself, that wasn't possible. They couldn't have been in Peru just four days. The crash seemed months ago. Halloween must have already come and gone. Thanksgiving, too. Christmas. New Year's. It would be winter back in the States, with snowstorms, sledding, hot chocolate by the fireplace...

The thought of snow brought tears to Jodie's eyes. What a luxury to be cold! She imagined her mother in her studio, where she sat gazing out through the big window at snow sifting down through the bare oak branches onto the white lawn. She would be wondering about Jodie, Matt, and Rus—where they were, what they were doing, whether they were even alive. Jodie knew that her mom would mobilize the American government, the Air Force, the Coast Guard, the Marines... Dad would spread the word among the missions, the Peruvian government, the army, the rainforest Indians...

Her parents would never give up—Jodie knew that without a doubt.

Matt had almost managed to fall asleep when he heard Jodie and Rus whispering in the dark.

"You think we'll make it?"—that was Jodie's voice.

"Make it home?" Rus shot back. "Yeah, we'll make it home."

"I mean will we, you know, *survive?*"

Rus hesitated.

Hearing that pause, Matt almost demanded to hear the answer.

Then Rus said, "Don't be a jerk. Of *course* we'll survive."

"But how?"

"Heck if I know. All I know is we will."

Matt felt pleased to hear Rus sounding so confident.

"But are you *sure?*"

Suddenly Rus's tone of voice changed: "Look— we've got lots of problems without you bugging yourself to death. Save your energy."

"I'm just kinda worried—"

"I know you are. That's the problem."

"But what if we *don't* survive?" Jodie asked.

The only answer to Jodie's question was the whirring, clicking, and chittering of bugs all around them in the forest.

28

The next morning they set off again, leaving their campsite well before sunrise. At first Rus wondered why they should rush off; they could take their time. Then he decided there was no point in lingering. They had no sleeping bags to roll up, no tent to dismantle, no gear to pack. Breakfast was water from the river and took maybe fifteen seconds to consume. All they had to do after that was climb aboard the raft.

They all felt so tired that they didn't talk much. Rus poked at the river bottom with a pole. Jodie and Matt lay on the raft's plastic floor and dozed. They waited for the sun to clear the canopy. They'd be too cool for a while, then too warm. And hungry. Hungry. Hungry.

Rus baited the bent suture needle with a piece of piranha skin from yesterday's catch. *Better this than my own flesh,* he thought, but he'd do whatever worked. He tossed the line into the water.

Within a few minutes, he'd caught a fish. Bright silver: sleek, shiny, and longer than a piranha.

"What is it?" Matt demanded.

"I have no idea," he answered. "I'm not picky." Rus sliced it open, gutted it, skinned it, and ate the meat right off the bones. Jodie and Matt stared at him the whole time, their expressions revealing a mix of disgust and envy.

"Want some?" Rus asked, holding out the skeleton.

Jodie turned away.

Matt held out both hands like someone fending off a blow.

Rus shook his head. "I know this isn't a chili dog," he told him, "but you guys better eat *something.*"

Neither of them answered.

They probably wouldn't eat unless he served the meal on gold-rimmed china. Let them starve, then. *Survival of the fittest.*

Experimenting, Rus discovered that Double-O plain gut suture worked best—strong enough to hold a good-sized fish but light enough to be invisible underwater. Triple-O nylon seemed good, too, though a bit light for larger fish. Double- and triple-O nylon suture worked fairly well if the fish were hungry enough to ignore the black filament. Other kinds of suture weren't so effective. The needles on the suture also made a difference. Fifteen millimeter needles were the easiest to bend. Tens were too small to make good hooks; twenties were too stiff. Rus experimented with all sorts of combinations to figure out what would catch the most fish. You learned what you could and then put the knowledge where you needed it. Sink or swim.

"Hey!" Matt yelled, startling Rus.

He pulled his attention back to the raft, the river, and his cousins. He'd caught another fish.

"A big silver one!" Jodie hollered.

"Here?" Rus said as he pulled out his catch.

"Yechhh!"

"You're missing a real feast."

"No way!" Matt shouted. "I'll wait till Dad can fix me some gringo food."

Rus couldn't believe Matt's thick-headedness. Jodie's, too. It might be days before they reached safety. How could they skip some real food now in favor of an imaginary meal in the future? Were they so accustomed to Jack and Penny waiting on them that they couldn't grasp the reality confronting them?

What amazed him most of all was the confidence they showed in their parents. Not that he doubted their commitment to Jodie and Matt. But to feel sure that Jack and Penny would overcome such difficult obstacles and brave so many dangers. . . It seemed unfamiliar and strange.

What must it feel like, Rus wondered, to be so sure of someone else's love?

29

Lying face up, Jodie tried to ignore the discomfort of her sunburned skin rubbing against the lumpy raft; to distract herself, she concentrated on the sky. Vast clouds billowed overhead. They were white and brilliant now but would turn slate gray within a few hours. She'd worry about that later. Right now she felt too weary and sore to think about something as far off as the afternoon. Her head throbbed. She felt sick to her stomach.

She was aware of Rus somewhere to her left, fishing. The raft shifted and creaked when he moved. Now and then she heard the hook go *plip* when he tossed it overboard.

Jodie filled her canteen from the river and took a long guzzle of the tea-colored liquid. Then she held the plastic bottle out to her cousin.

Rus glanced over and said, "Not now."

"Don't thank me or anything."

"Okay."

He had just caught a fish—something that resembled a big sardine—and he now set to work preparing and eating it. Slicing off the pearl-colored flesh with a scalpel, Rus threw his head back, dangled strips of raw meat over his open mouth, and dropped them in. Jodie could barely stand to watch. She craved food more than anything, yet somehow she couldn't tolerate the sight of Rus's meal. She certainly couldn't force herself to eat these creatures from the muddy river. Feeling so torn gave her a splitting headache.

Rus, though, simply gobbled anything he caught.

"How can you eat that stuff?" Jodie asked suddenly.

He snorted. "Simple! There's nothing else!"

111

"But isn't it, like, *gross?*"

"Of course," Rus said with a laugh. "Totally, positively, absolutely gross."

"Then how can you do it?"

"'Cause I'm gonna do whatever it takes to get out of here, Princess. And eating this slime isn't nearly as gross as starving to death."

Jodie turned away as Rus started sucking on the fish's skeleton.

How could he feel so positive, she wondered, about his own ability to survive? Hardships didn't seem a nightmare to Rus, just a series of obstacles to work around. Rus never seemed to doubt that he'd emerge from this ordeal. He admitted he wasn't sure how, but he knew he'd succeed. Why? Jodie couldn't even guess. Maybe Rus had been through such rough times that the rainforest wasn't so uncomfortable. The heat wasn't so hot as for Jodie and Matt. The rain wasn't so wet. The bugs weren't so itchy. The thorns weren't so sharp.

Something occurred to her just then. Was it possible, Jodie asked herself, that Rus's attitude worked to his advantage? And maybe to Matt's and Jodie's, too? While Jodie and Matt noticed every little problem, danger, and discomfort, Rus somehow focused simply on making it out of the rainforest alive. And it occurred to her that no matter how obnoxious this attitude made Rus most of the time—as if he alone knew what to do!—it might help them all get through their ordeal. He'd tune out everything but whatever had to be done. He'd ignore the growing likelihood that they'd never make it home. Rus would survive.

It was as if his confidence in himself was a fire, a private campfire glowing within his mind, that somehow lit up the gloom all around them.

112

30

Something jolted the raft.
Instantly alert, Matt forced himself onto all fours.
"What is it!"

The raft trembled. Matt heard an odd stuttering noise, then a thud. At that moment, the platform tipped steeply to one side. He barely managed to hang on. He heard Jodie and Rus hollering but he couldn't even pay attention; all he could do was struggle to keep from getting dumped into the river.

"Hey!"—Jodie's voice, full of fear.

The raft grunted as if in pain. Was it sinking?

No, Matt realized, it wasn't sinking—just tilting. But that was bad enough. Grabbing at the plastic floor and the branches underneath, he could barely keep hold. His feet kicked and splashed in the water. If his hands lost their grip, he'd fall right in. The thought terrified him: he could probably swim to shore, but what about the piranhas? What if the raft fell apart? How would they survive without the raft? Matt clutched the platform so hard that his fingertips tore through the plastic floor to the branches beyond.

"Rus—stay over there!" Jodie shouted. "Keep it balanced!"

"No, it'll—"

"Stay put!"

Matt didn't know what to do. All he could think about was the piranhas waiting for him in the water. . .

The raft didn't sink or fall apart. Once the kids succeeded in towing it to shore, Jodie understood what had happened. One of the water-jug pontoons had come loose, angling the raft and nearly sliding everyone overboard. The stress on the platform had dislodged a second jug and nearly knocked off a third. How? Jodie wasn't sure. Even Matt couldn't explain it. Maybe the raft had struck a sunken log. Scary: the whole raft could have gotten pulled apart. Fortunately it hadn't. The platform was intact, and none of the loops of stretchy rubber had torn. The big problem now was hitching the jugs back to the platform.

"Here," Jodie said, picking up one of the loose jugs.

"Stretch that tourniquet stuff," Matt said.

"Give it to me," Rus ordered.

"Rus and I are stronger," Jodie told Matt, "so we'll do the pulling. You position the jug."

"But I designed it!" Matt protested.

"Who cares who designed it?" Rus grumbled. "Let's just fix it."

They argued for a while. No one seemed clear-headed or patient, and they kept getting in each other's way. Getting along grew more difficult than doing the task itself. After many disagreements, Jodie held the jug while Rus and Matt pulled the rubber in opposite directions. Eventually they created an O big enough to hold the jug; Jodie shoved it into place. "Seems okay," she said, testing it.

"Sure better be," Rus said.

Then Jodie and Rus hoisted the raft and set it back into the river.

"Good as new," Matt announced.

Watching the raft rest calmly on the water, Jodie felt a huge sense of relief. What would have happened, she wondered, if they hadn't managed to repair it? What could they have done? What would have become of them? Luckily they *had* repaired it. The raft rested safe and solid in the water. Staring at it with pride, Jodie couldn't imagine anything more beautiful than this tangle of sticks, wire, tape, rubber, and plastic. "Let's hope *that* never happens again," she said.

Yet despite her relief, Jodie felt so tired that her legs buckled suddenly, forcing her to sit on the muddy bank.

"You okay?" Rus asked her.

Leaning forward, she put her face in her hands. "I don't feel good."

Matt crouched beside her. "What's wrong?"

"I don't know." She touched her head and neck. "I'm so hot," she said. "Maybe too much sun."

"I guess you're right about the sunburn," Rus said.

Jodie sat there, dizzy and weak, for a long time.

Matt felt more and more worried about Jodie's sunburn. She looked awful—red and puffy—and she seemed to be running out of energy. Worse yet, Matt himself was, too. At the rate they were going, they'd get cooked to a crisp. But what choice did they have, really, except to set off again in the raft?

"Guys," he said. "We've got to protect ourselves."

He expected Rus to tease or hassle him. Instead, his cousin only asked, "You got something in mind?"

"Maybe sun block," Matt said.

"I brought some," Jodie said, "but it's back inside the Badger's cargo hold.

Matt said, "If we had some cloth, we could wear it like ponchos."

"But we don't," Rus noted, "so we can't."

"How about plastic?" Matt asked.

"You and your plastic," Rus grumbled.

"We could make plastic ponchos."

"Plastic is transparent, dummy."

"Oh, yeah—I forgot."

"Good try," said Jodie. She forced herself up, muttering, then looked suddenly at her hands. Gray mud covered both of her palms. Staring at the mess, she said, "Home-made sun block! We'll smear mud on our skin."

Matt grimaced. "Yuck!"

"No go," Rus said. "It'll dry out and fall right off. It'll be twenty times more trouble than it's worth."

Matt felt more and more discouraged. They couldn't stay there much longer; they had to keep moving. As nice as it felt, they couldn't just hang out in the shade forever.

Which suddenly gave him an idea. Matt staggered up the riverbank and into the forest. It felt almost cool in there, for the great canopy overhead blocked almost all of the sunlight. He shouted, "Hey!"

Jodie and Rus gazed up at him.

"Tell me this: will I get sunburned *here*?"

"Of course not," Rus answered wearily.

"Right!" Matt said. "And why's that?"

"'Cause you're in the shade," Jodie stated.

"Good thinking. So let's just take some of this shade *with* us."

"What are you talking about?"

He motioned toward the palm leaves slanting his head. "Shade," Matt said. "Plain ol' shade."

It didn't take long to figure things out. Matt sized up the situation and suggested the basic structure. Using the tourniquet rubber already stretched around the empty water jugs, they strapped big sticks onto each of the raft's four corners to form the vertical posts for a canopy. Tying four more sticks sideways at the top of the posts—they used jungle vines as string—formed a horizontal support. From there it was easy to create a roof of palm leaves. The result was light, fairly strong, and dense enough to screen out most of the sunlight.

"It's like a canopy bed!" Jodie exclaimed.

"Just what every princess needs," Rus said.

Matt was delighted. Now they'd sail down the river in style! He didn't have enough energy to jump around in delight, but he felt pleased anyway, and on impulse he hugged his sister.

Rus stood watching.

Then Jodie, looking over Matt's shoulder, yelled, "You guys! The raft!"

Matt looked up.

The raft had drifted five or ten feet downstream.

"Get it!" Rus shouted.

Splashing into the water, Jodie reached the raft, grabbed it, and towed it back to shore. "That was dumb," she said, holding it steady. "We've *got* to be more careful."

No one had the energy to react; Matt and Rus simply stared at her.

Shaken and exhausted, Matt climbed back on board. He couldn't believe how good it felt to set off and start down the river again. The raft would protect them. The raft would carry them to safety.

Yet he couldn't relax. The raft stuttered and grunted almost as if struggling to speak. Matt listened closely to the message but couldn't tell what it meant.

31

L ook!"
Jodie turned to see what Matt had spotted. Ges-
turing frantically, he motioned toward something
ahead and to the left.

"What is it?"

"A canoe!"

Matt must have been mistaken, Jodie told herself.
Rain had been falling for most of the past hour, and the
storm had just recently started to let up. It wasn't easy to
see through the lingering downpour. She saw what he
meant—a gray thing near the riverbank—but she couldn't
believe he'd really spotted a canoe. A log, maybe. A
low, gray piece of trunk.

Then Jodie saw that he was right. The tapered
front and back, the carved-out body, the two low wooden
seats: it really was a canoe.

A canoe.

"Let's get out of here," Rus said firmly. *"Fast."*

"What!" she exclaimed. "Let's check it out!" She
felt her heart pounding. If they could just find some
people, they'd be all right. Food, safety, and a quick trip
to Dad would quickly follow. They'd soon be on their
way home.

While Jodie used her pole to shove the raft toward
the riverbank, Rus shoved it in the opposite direction.
The raft trembled, rotating slowly. Then, though Rus
was stronger than Jodie, it somehow started drifting
toward the shore.

Rus pulled his pole out. "This is nuts!"

"Definitely a canoe," Matt stated.

Jodie looked more closely. It wasn't like an
American canoe, with a wide middle and high ends. Ten
or twelve feet long but little more than eighteen inches

118

wide, it must have been a dugout. It rode low in the water—so low that water had swamped it. Was it abandoned? Damaged?

"Hey!" she shouted, aiming the word at the forest. "We're here!"

"What are you *doing?*" Rus asked, lowering his voice in dismay.

She ignored him. "Here! We need help!"

"Stop it!"

"Hola!" she yelled. Then, not knowing how to say "Help" in Spanish, she hollered the only other words she knew: *"Buenos días! Gracias! Adios!"*

Rus clapped a hand over Jodie's mouth. "What are you doing!"

"Get your hands *off* me!" Furious, Jodie struggled with Rus. She almost punched him but didn't want to make him even angrier. "Leave me alone!"

"Stop screaming."

She sat abruptly. How could anyone be so stupid! "Our only hope," Jodie told him, "is to find someone who'll help us."

Rus huffed in annoyance. "Right—the rescuers."

"Or anyone else."

"Anyone?" Rus asked, his voice cracking.

"Anyone who'll help us," Jodie said with a shrug.

"Yeah, right. The jungle is full of folks waiting to do their next good deed."

"What makes you think they're not?"

Rus guffawed. "'Cause they're people, that's why."

"That doesn't mean they're bad."

"I didn't say bad. Just selfish," Rus said. "People take care of themselves."

"Fine—but they'll help us anyway."

"Yeah? Tell me why. Tell me just one reason."

"I don't know why, but I know they will," Jodie said.

"You just think that," Rus said.

119

"No, it's true."

Rus suddenly lost his temper. "You think that 'cause you don't know any better. 'Cause you've never had a rough day in your life. 'Cause nobody's ever done anything bad to you. Ever."

"That's not true."

"Nobody's done anything as bad as what those Indians'll do," he stated.

"Oh, stop!" Jodie told him. "You don't know that."

"We can't take chances."

"It's our *only* chance." Jodie turned to Matt, who looked uneasy and afraid as this argument went on and on. "Matt, listen to me," she said. "We can't keep going like this—alone. We have to get some help. Doesn't that make sense?"

She saw him glance anxiously at Rus. "I guess so," Matt said.

"Don't get fooled," Rus told Matt. "It's too big a gamble."

Matt looked awful—as if he'd sort of folded up into himself. "I don't know what you guys want!" he hollered. "Just leave me alone!"

32

They beached the raft—this time pulling it onto the riverbank so it couldn't drift away again—and they scrambled into the forest. Matt didn't want to go with them, but he didn't want to stay alone with the raft, either, so he went along.

All for nothing. No sign of a village. No sign even of a trail in the forest.

Returning to the river, Rus let Jodie go ahead. Then he waited for Matt. "Why are you doing what she says?" he asked.

"I'm not," Matt told him uneasily.

"Sure you are. She snaps her fingers and you come running like a puppy."

"I do not!"

"Don't kid yourself, Matt. You'd do anything she asked."

"She's my sister."

"That's my whole point," Rus said. "She's your sister. Are you gonna let your sister boss you around?"

Matt felt more and more frustrated. "Leave me alone."

"Are you?"

Matt walked off.

Rus grabbed him by the shoulder. "Listen," Rus said, "this isn't a game. We're not talking about who's the best inventor."

"I know that."

"We're talking about getting home alive."

"Rus, I *know.*"

"Good. 'Cause if we get nabbed by the Indians, we're dead."

Matt pulled away from Rus and stomped off.

121

Then, just as Rus left, Jodie cornered Matt. "We've always worked together."

Matt nodded.

"Matt and Jodie, Jodie and Matt."

He nodded again but wouldn't meet her gaze.

"So why are you ganging up with Rus?"

"I don't know what you're talking about."

"Yes you do." She stood there with a hand on her hip, just like Mom.

Matt shrugged. "You're not my mother."

"No, but I'm your sister, and I'm older than you are," she snapped, "so I'm in charge. Mom and Dad would've put me in charge."

Matt forced a laugh. "Well, hey—if we're doing this by age, *Rus* is in charge, 'cause *he's* the oldest!" At once he felt uncomfortable: Matt didn't really want Rus in charge. He stammered, "Who says *anyone's* in charge?"

"That's just the point," Jodie told him. "We've got to work together."

"Fine." Matt avoided her gaze.

"Come on—don't do stuff behind my back. We're all in the same mess."

He looked up at Jodie. The sparkle in her eyes reassured him, and her smile was the same smile that always cheered him when he felt bad. "Okay," Matt said.

But Matt didn't know what to do. He felt shoved around by both his cousin and his sister. He didn't like having them angry at him. He didn't like having to choose between one and the other. He especially didn't like having to figure out who was right at such a difficult time: Rus, who was so confident and tough; or Jodie, who was so supportive and kind.

33

Dazed and clumsy, they set off again. Jodie caught herself making stupid mistakes—first leaving a box of supplies behind, then dropping her pole into the river. She felt weak and sick to her stomach. Her arms ached. Her head throbbed. She couldn't imagine another day's struggle. Most of all she couldn't see how she'd stay patient with Rus, who was even grouchier than usual.

At least they weren't totally without food. Once Rus had gotten the hang of fishing with such crude equipment, he had increased his catch to at least half a dozen fish per day. They were small—not more than a few ounces apiece. Piranhas, mostly, which were flat and lean. Some thicker gray-green fish, too: Rus said they were bass. Then Jodie tried her luck and caught something so shiny that it looked like polished silver. Not exactly a feast. The idea of eating raw fish still disgusted her. Sometimes she thought she'd actually rather die than eat raw fish. Yet she was so hungry now that she didn't care. She sampled some piranha and decided it tasted okay. Rainforest sushi. . . Then, startling herself, she gobbled it, scraping her teeth against the flesh and sucking on the bones.

"The Princess decides to eat with the commoners!" Rus said with a laugh.

"Oh, shut up." But Jodie didn't really care what Rus thought or said. She felt too relieved to have something—anything—to eat.

Matt kept wondering about the situation. Maybe Indians *did* lurk in the forest, waiting to ambush the raft as it floated past. Or maybe they'd do everything they could to help the kids. Matt wasn't sure. Everything Dad had explained about these people made them sound so friendly, but was it possible that *some* of the Indians were mean? Matt found it easy to imagine them barefoot, dressed only in loincloths, sneaking among the trees, signaling each other with fake bird calls, then crashing through the bushes, splashing out to the raft, and capturing the kids.

He spotted a bright blue spot among the leaves. "Hey!" Matt shouted. "Over there!" War paint? Indians hiding in the forest?

"What is it?" Jodie demanded.

He looked again and realized what he'd really seen: a big blue butterfly on a branch. "Oh, nothing." He felt like an idiot.

She asked, "Are you okay?"

"I'm fine."

Jodie reached out and touched Matt's forehead. "You've got a fever."

"I'm okay," Matt told her. "Just kinda tired."

He didn't tell her that his whole body buzzed with fatigue. Luckily, what he'd seen had been harmless. Feeling so terrible, though, how would he manage to escape if the Indians *did* attack?

Rus stared at Jodie and Matt as they dozed on the raft that afternoon. The greatest luxury in the world, he decided, would be to kick free of them. It was hard enough to put up with these two during ordinary times; now, stuck with each other during a crisis, they were almost intolerable. Matt's pathetic weakness. Jodie's stuck-up attitudes. How could he stay patient?

Yet whenever he thought of bolting into the forest, Rus couldn't make even the first move. He felt too tired to risk it. His head hurt constantly. His left arm ached from the swollen scratches. He couldn't imagine abandoning the fishing gear and the other supplies, no matter how meager.

Something else held him back, though, a reluctance that Rus hadn't expected to feel. Matt was incredibly annoying, but he'd thought up many of the best ideas so far: the basic raft design, the addition of the jugs as pontoons, the use of sutures as fishing line. What would this goofy kid think up next? And Jodie, though frustrating in her own way, had made some break-throughs, too: finding the football fruit, realizing that they could go fishing, and figuring out that suture needles could be fishhooks. She had also managed to prod everyone into putting up with each other, which had made this whole raft trip possible. So maybe it wasn't such a good idea, Rus decided, to be rid of them quite yet.

Watching Matt and Jodie, Rus felt still another emotion he hadn't anticipated. He felt shaken by how awful his cousins looked. Their skin had turned orange-red from sunburn. So many bug bites speckled their bodies that they looked as if they'd caught the chicken pox. Jodie's shoulder-length brown hair lay around her in filthy strings. Matt's short hair was spiky and knotted. Both kids looked dirty, bruised, and sunken-eyed.

Rus wondered if he looked as bad as they did. From his reflection in the water, he thought maybe so. But at least he didn't simply pass out, he told himself, like a couple of toddlers after visiting the zoo.

Weaklings, Rus thought. Spoiled brats.

Yet a growing concern nagged at him while he watched Matt and Jodie sleep. Rus watched and waited, careful not to waken them.

34

Someone's there!" Matt shouted, pointing to a glint in the foliage.

"What is it?" Jodie asked.

"Get down!" Rus told them. He shoved Matt till he squatted on the raft.

Matt couldn't tell what he saw. Something made of metal: a shield, a helmet?

He felt a surge of panic. Maybe some Indians? He couldn't see anyone. . . What should he do, run and hide? Or holler and plead for help?

"Hey!" Jodie shouted. *"Hola!"*

Rus shoved her. "Stop it!"

"Buenos días!"

Matt watched with growing alarm as Jodie and Rus started to struggle.

"Don't be an idiot!" Rus yelled, trying to cup a hand over Jodie's mouth.

"Get your mitts off me!"

Gazing toward the opposite riverbank, Matt couldn't see anything now.

Then Jodie, breaking free of Rus, ran ahead and leaped into the river. She splashed in, waded deeper, and swam toward the other side.

Matt stared, too terrified to speak. The piranhas. . .

Just a few dozen strokes got her across. Jodie staggered out of the water, walked into the bushes, and disappeared. A moment later she returned, holding a black-and-silver object. "It's a pot!" she hollered. She raised it for them to see. "An old beat-up cooking pot."

"Great," Rus said. After a moment he shouted, "Now get back here, okay?"

Jodie walked back to the river and leaped in. She swam across and struggled out, streaming water. "There's people here!" she exclaimed. "This proves it!"

"That was real dumb," Rus said as she approached.

"We'll find them soon."

"That's what I'm worried about."

Matt couldn't believe how pleased Jodie looked.

"And look," she said. "Now we have a pot!" She held it up.

Matt felt surprised by the sight of it. Aluminum!

Rus shrugged. "At least it's too small for boiling kids," he said. "Meanwhile, you're lucky the piranhas didn't gobble you first."

Rus was furious that Jodie had risked revealing their presence to the Indians. What dumb move would she make next? "After today," he announced after they'd launched the raft and set off again, "we'll travel only at night."

He'd expected Jodie to object, and she did: "Are you nuts? At night?"

"It's the only sensible option."

"There's nothing sensible about it. We won't be able to see—"

"And no one will see *us*," he noted.

Crouched on the raft, she stared at Rus with feverish intensity. "I don't get it!" she exclaimed. "Isn't the whole point that we *want* to get seen?"

"Yeah, but only by the right folks."

"Meaning?"

"Rescuers," he stated. He couldn't believe she'd fail to grasp something so obvious. "Not a bunch of Indians."

Jodie stood, wobbling the raft. "But that's who lives here!" she shouted. "That's who'll rescue us!"

"Stop hollering."

"I'll holler if I want!"

Rus turned to Matt. *"Talk* with her," he told him. "Maybe she'll listen to *you."*

Matt gazed back, looking helpless. "Jodie," Matt said, "maybe Rus is right."

Rus hoped this comment might persuade her, but it only infuriated Jodie even worse. "Don't pit us against each other," she told Rus. "He's too young to know better. But you, Rus—*you're* old enough to know—"

"I *do* know."

"—that we can't pull this off alone." The raft trembled from her shifting weight.

"Sit down," Rus told her. "And stop shouting!"

Now she started bellowing. "Help! Indians, come rescue us! We need help!"

Rus reached out, trying to force her down, but Jodie swung at him.

"Jodie—stop it!"

He leaned closer, grabbing her shoulders.

When the raft shifted, he lost his balance, struggled to stay upright, and toppled to the left. "Jodie—"

Was she shoving Rus off the raft, Matt asked himself, shocked by what he saw—or was she trying to keep Rus from falling?

Matt couldn't make sense of what was happening. He'd seen lots of arguments between Rus and Jodie but never one this bad. They screamed, they yelled, they accused each other of terrible things. They hit, even.

It terrified him to think they'd get hurt. Someone might even get killed.

Then what would happen? How would Matt survive in this place if he didn't have his sister and his cousin to protect him?

Matt saw Jodie reach toward Rus. He struggled with her.

Was she shoving him off the raft—or trying to keep him from falling?

* * *

Suddenly Rus was in the water. The water rushed into his nose and ears and mouth, he couldn't breathe, he could only struggle with the water. He reached the surface and felt the air hit his face, but gasping got him a mouthful of water, not air, and he struggled even harder when the coughing started. His lungs felt ready to burst. Rus clawed for anything to get him out.

There was nothing solid, only water. Water gagged his mouth. Water plugged his ears. Water blinded his eyes. Water bound his hands and feet. Water filled his throat. Rus groped for the surface but found only water.

I'm drowning, Mom had told him as her body filled with fluid.

Is this how she felt? Rus wondered.

The river tangled him and dragged him down. Rus grew heavy, heavy as stone. *You're such a millstone.*

Sink or swim.

Flailing, he sank. Bubbles fled through his mouth.

Something scraped his shoulder. Fish? Piranhas coming to devour him?

A great shadowy shape loomed, drew near, and caught hold of him.

Rus had no strength for resisting. He fought back anyway.

The shape grabbed him, grappled with him, overpowered him.

Panicking, Rus felt the air rush from his lungs. *I'm drowning.*

Isn't there something I could do?

Well thanks Sweetie but I don't know what that would be.

Then something took hold of Rus so firmly that he couldn't resist, and the darkness swamping him diminished.

35

Jodie couldn't get Rus back onto the raft. Gasping for breath, she could barely keep him from sliding underwater. Hanging onto Rus with one hand while clutching the platform with the other took all her strength.

"Help me!" Jodie shouted.

"I'm trying!" Matt called back.

She could see that her brother's efforts to pull Rus out weren't succeeding—Matt was too weak or tired or sick to help. Jodie felt Rus slipping from her grasp. He didn't seem aware of her, yet he struggled, flailing, till his body was impossible to control. Jodie's arms cramped from the effort.

Rus was drowning. He'd drown and sink to the bottom...

Jodie almost screamed in fear and sadness at the thought of Rus's fate. Fear, because she dreaded what would become of her if Rus died. Sadness, because she dreaded what would become of *Rus*.

But she didn't scream. Instead, she hollered to Matt: "Grab a pole!"

Did he understand?

"Push the—raft!" Jodie called out. "Toward the—shore!" If they could just reach shallow water...

Clutching one of the poles, Matt started shoving. Jodie couldn't tell if his efforts made a difference or not. She knew only that she couldn't hold Rus much longer.

Then she felt her toes touch the bottom. Once she could push down with both feet, she swung the raft around, waded toward the forest, and pulled Rus part way out. Then Matt hopped off the raft and, splashing toward the riverbank, helped Jodie with Rus.

Together they dragged him onto the muddy shore.

* * *

Matt was terrified that Rus had drowned. He didn't move much, only twitched, lying there in a twisted heap. "Don't die, don't die, don't die!" Matt shouted, and he tugged on Rus's arm as if to keep him from leaving.

Jodie was scared, too, Matt could tell. But she kept moving—checking his mouth and throat, shoving him onto his side, taking his pulse.

Rus jolted hard, rolled to one side, and threw up. Water, lots of water.

Matt backed off, disgusted, yet he was thrilled to hear Rus start coughing.

He was alive.

Rus couldn't figure it out. Why would they bother? He wasn't even their real brother, just a pretend brother, and they didn't even like him. They treated him as a burden, a millstone, something that would drag them down, down, down to the bottom.

Rus shivered as he recalled the water grabbing him, shoving him around, battering him. The river's fist pounding his face. Then hands catching hold of him: not the stinking water-hands, but real hands. Jodie's hands. Matt's hands. They pulled at him, held him, helped him out of the river.

Why? Lying there, dazed, he couldn't find the answer. Why would they have risked it, jumped into the muddy river full of razor-toothed fish, rather than clinging safely to the raft?

And not just one of them had jumped in. Both. They'd rescued him. *Him*—Rus Cooper.

"You okay?" Jodie asked Rus.

"Just great," he muttered.

"Well, at least you're not dead."

131

"I'm not so sure." He rested his face in the palms of both hands. For a long time he didn't move and didn't speak.

Jodie wanted to reassure him, soothe him, comfort him. This had been such a close call—she felt amazed and relieved that he'd made it through alive. Then she recalled the argument right before Rus fell into the river. Surprising herself, she blasted him: "Don't feel sorry for yourself, okay? That was your own fault."

"My fault?"

"Fighting with me like that—no wonder you fell overboard!"

"You *pushed* me," Rus said.

"I did not!" Jodie hollered.

"Sure you did."

"You've got a lot of nerve, Rus Cooper! *Pushed* you? I should've let you sink straight to the bottom—"

"So why didn't you?" he asked suddenly. "Why'd you save me?"

Jodie started to speak but couldn't. She wanted to lash out at Rus, to clobber him for his nerviness, but she couldn't even speak. All she could think about was what his rough life had done to him.

"Maybe you shouldn't've saved me," Rus said.

"No," she told him. "I wanted to."

"You *wanted* to?"

"I didn't even think about it. I just did it."

"Yeah, but *why?"*

She hesitated. She kept remembering how scared she'd felt when Rus fell in. How terrified that he'd die. "Because you're my brother!" she blurted.

"But I'm not," Rus said. "Not really."

"You *are."*

"Just because your parents adopted me doesn't mean—"

"You're my brother."

"I'm your cousin. I'm just your cousin."

"Down deep you're my brother," Jodie told him. "Here," she said, thumping her chest with her right fist. "*Here*. You're my brother because that's what I want you to be."

Rus looked confused. "Jodie—"

"I couldn't let anything bad happen to you."

"Jodie—"

"Not after all you've been through."

"Hey!"

Jodie turned abruptly. Matt, not Rus, had shouted. "What's the matter?"

"The raft!"

Jodie glanced toward the water's edge just a few feet away.

The raft wasn't there.

"Where'd it go?" she asked. She looked up and down the riverbank but couldn't see the raft.

"There!" Matt shouted.

Hundreds of yards downstream—so far down that Jodie couldn't even feel sure she'd spotted it at all—the raft was drifting away.

Part Four

The Forest

36

Matt watched in alarm as Jodie ran off. At first, slipping and skidding in the mud, she followed the riverbank. Soon bushes blocked her path, so she scrambled up the bank into the forest. He lost sight of her soon after that.

"Jodie!" he bellowed.

Only a fragment of her answer reached him:

"—back!—"

"Don't leave!"

She shouted something, but Matt couldn't understand a word.

Seeing her run away terrified him, yet he *wanted* her to leave—Jodie was their only hope for rescuing the raft. And if they lost the raft. . .

Five minutes passed. Ten. Where was Jodie?

A deep chill came over him. *He was alone.*

Then, turning, he realized he wasn't.

Rus crouched a few yards away on the riverbank.

Rus forced himself upright, took two steps, and toppled over. With his hands and knees drenched in mud, he stood again and fell almost at once. His head pounded. His lungs felt raw and torn. He started to cough and couldn't stop.

He was aware of Matt racing around, hollering about the raft, and bellowing to Jodie. The raft—where was the raft? Rus glanced about but couldn't make sense of what he saw. Mud, water. . . He couldn't spot the raft.

A wave of nausea hit Rus so suddenly that he barely had time to crouch before he started vomiting. For a moment Rus thought he'd pass out. His head spun. He lay down in the mud and rested against the angle of the riverbank. The pillow of mud felt deliciously warm.

Where was the raft?
The next thing he knew, the forest had grown dark.

Jodie pushed her way quickly through the foliage. Branches thrashed her. Vines and dead branches tripped her. Falling time after time, she scraped her knees, arms, hands, and face. Yet she never slowed—she couldn't risk losing the raft. No matter what it took, Jodie told herself, she had to find the raft.

She should have caught up with it easily, she told herself; the water flowed so slowly that Jodie could have outrun it. But this forest was an obstacle course. She had to work her way around the big trees, between the little ones, through bushes, and over thickets of weeds and ferns. Within minutes her bare legs were bleeding from scrapes, scratches, and slashes that the plants inflicted on her. She kept running anyway. If they lost the raft. . .

Now and then Jodie pushed her way back to the river. She glanced downstream, upstream, and across the water hoping to spot the raft. She couldn't see it anywhere. Then at once she ran along the riverbank or else, when it was too narrow, she headed up the bank and into the forest once again.

She couldn't imagine what would happen if she failed to find the raft. It wasn't just the raft itself; they'd lose all their equipment, too. *Then* what would they do?

Impulsively, Jodie went down the bank, waded into the water, and dived in. She stroked forward in a strong crawl. If she couldn't chase down the raft on foot, she'd swim after it. Jodie clawed through the water for two or three minutes. Where was the raft? She couldn't spot it.

There!

She swam again, stroking hard.

But on reaching it, Jodie saw that this wasn't the raft at all—only a couple of big floating branches, dense with leaves, that she'd found in the water. She clung,

138

panting, to this tangle of debris. She glanced around but couldn't see the raft anywhere.

Something bumped against her right leg. Jodie twitched in alarm. A fish? An eel? Her own words came to her: *They won't bite you unless you're wounded.* Jodie pulled her hand out of the water and stared at it. Five or six little cuts criss-crossed her palm. . .

At once she set off, thrashing toward the riverbank.

Streaming water, Jodie stumbled ashore. She felt more and more afraid. Her heart pounded, her lungs ached, and every muscle in her body told her to give up. The situation was hopeless. Why resist? Why avoid the inevitable? They had lost their struggle. They were doomed. Lacking any gear, they'd succumb to hunger and exhaustion.

Something whispered, *Give up.*

Jodie fought the urge to obey. She felt so awful, it would be a relief to collapse and pass out. Would she die? Maybe so. The thought terrified her, but at least then she wouldn't burden Matt or Rus.

Thinking about her brothers jolted Jodie back to her senses. Matt was sick and feverish. Rus had nearly drowned. How could she ignore them when they needed her? She had no choice but to locate the raft.

So she pushed on, thrashing through the forest. It was harder to find her way now. The twilight was thick as smoke. Even when she worked her way down to the water again, Jodie couldn't get a clear view upstream or down.

She stood on the riverbank. Panting hard, she realized with a twinge of alarm that night had fallen. Jodie could see the stars above: clear, cold, white lights in the swath of sky visible between the trees. The trees themselves now appeared merely as silhouettes. At that moment she realized that even if the raft were only ten or twenty yards downstream, she'd never spot it.

"Matt?" she called out impulsively.

A bird called back: *Who-hoe!*

She stood still and listened. The forest echoed with animal sounds. Hoots. Hollers. Screeches. Buzzes. Cries. Nothing that resembled her name.

"Matt! Rus!" she hollered.

Somewhere in the river, a fish went *ploop!*

"Matt, where are you? Matt and Rus!"

Jodie fought the urge to cry. Holding her right hand at arm's length, she could scarcely see her fingers.

37

All night long Matt whimpered, muttered, and shook, his whole body aching with the urge to scream or sob or wail. Somehow he couldn't let go. He just lay on the leafy earth and trembled.

Until now, he'd thought they could bluff their way out of any setback. They'd solve problems. They'd make discoveries. They'd invent things. Now that was impossible. Everything they'd relied on was lost. Even Jodie was gone.

Whenever he dozed off for a few minutes, nightmares attacked him. Mosquitoes, ants, and centipedes swarmed over his skin. Birds swooped down and pecked his flesh. Piranhas leaped out of the river and tore him apart. Indians attacked with blowguns, arrows, and spears. Waking suddenly, Matt felt a moment's relief—none of these terrible things had happened. Then he realized where he was and felt his spirits sink again.

Jodie's absence worried him most of all. Where was she? Was she safe? Could he survive without her?

Only one thing kept Matt from panicking. *"Rus?"* he whispered.

"What," came the weary response in the dark.

"Are you okay?"

"Sure—just great."

Yet no matter how irritable his brother sounded, Matt felt better knowing that Rus was just a few feet away. Rus would protect him. Rus was thirteen and knew lots of stuff. Rus would figure out what to do.

Rus couldn't imagine how they'd survive this disaster. The raft was gone. All the gear, too. And Jodie.

"Rus?" said a feeble voice on his left.

"What," Rus answered. He couldn't take a deep breath without coughing. As if things weren't bad enough, he'd have to look after Dr. Invento—alone!

"I don't feel so good."

Rus nearly snapped at him, saying, *Welcome to the club!*—but he held off. He hesitated, then said, "Is there, like, something I could do?"

"I don't know," Matt said feebly.

No one spoke for a while. Bugs whined. Birds whooped. Some kind of creature made a sound like a pencil falling down a wooden staircase.

Staring into the darkness, Rus tried to see the little boy somewhere close by. He wanted to resent him. Matt was bogging him down, slowing Rus's efforts to save his own skin. Matt was a millstone— Yet somehow Rus couldn't hold Matt's weakness against him. Something stirred within him that he hadn't expected to feel. *You're my brother*, Jodie had told him, *because that's what I want you to be.* She must have meant it, too. Risking her own life, she'd jumped into the river and saved him. Why? Rus couldn't even guess. "Matt," he said.

"Yeah?"

"Are you getting cold?"

"Kinda."

Rus reached out to Matt till he touched his arm. "C'mere."

"What is it?"

"Let's snuggle up."

Scooting backwards, reclining against a tree, Rus guided Matt until the boy leaned back against Rus's chest. Rus wrapped his arms around his brother.

Waking with a jolt, Jodie forced herself up. Daybreak. Knives of sunlight stabbed through the canopy. She glanced around for Rus and Matt but saw she was alone. At once she recalled the reason for their absence, so she began the new day by doing what she'd done for hours the night before. "Hey, Rus! Matt!" Jodie hollered. "Where are you!"

Birds in the nearby trees fell silent, then gradually started calling out again.

No one shouted back to her.

Though exhausted and sore from all her cuts and bruises, Jodie set off at once. She headed upstream, following the riverbank whenever possible, toward the place where she had left Matt and Rus behind. Now and then she stopped to listen—she worried about missing her brothers in the forest—but she couldn't catch sight of them. "Matt! Rus!" she shouted over and over.

Still no answer.

Jodie arrived about an hour later at the spot where she had expected to find the boys. Or was she mistaken? The ferns, the vines, the saplings and trees. . . She could have been standing almost anywhere in the rainforest. She eased through a curtain of dangling vines and arrived at the riverbank.

"Matt?" she asked hesitantly. "Rus?"

No matter how carefully she looked, she couldn't find them.

"What is it!" Matt hollered, waking suddenly.

He struggled to force himself upright. He couldn't recognize the place. Big trees. . . Tangles of plants. . . Rus sat nearby against a moss-covered trunk. Matt couldn't see him well, his eyes were so puffy.

"Hey," Rus said quietly. "It's okay."

"Where are we?"

"Still in Peru. The jungle."

"Where's Jodie?" Matt asked.

"Out there someplace," Rus replied.

Matt's spirits sank. He started to remember the day before—Rus nearly drowning, the raft floating off, Jodie chasing after it. They were still lost. Matt felt so weak he could barely prop himself up. "I'm hungry," he told Rus.

"I wish I could help you," Rus said, "but we're kinda short on supplies." He held both hands out, palms empty.

Matt suddenly remembered how they'd lost all their equipment. "What are we gonna do?" he asked.

"I'm not sure yet." After a moment's hesitation Rus said, "The one thing I'm sure of is—we've gotta stay clear of the Indians."

Indians, Matt thought, unsure if he should feel dread or hope.

Exhausted, Rus tried to figure out how he and Matt could stay alive. He wasn't sure, but somehow they'd keep going. *Survival of the fittest.* They'd eat fish Rus would skewer with a homemade spear. They'd trap birds with improvised snares. Maybe they'd build another raft—tear down saplings and lash them together with vines and, traveling only at night, they'd float downstream till they reached civilization. If they could locate Jodie, all the better. If they needed to head off alone, so be it. Rus would do anything necessary to keep himself and Matt alive.

So he sized up the situation as well as possible. He scouted the area, looked for fruit to eat, noted any fallen trees to make into a raft. He tried to figure out a way to escape the net of problems tightening around them.

Sitting on a log while Matt dozed nearby, he couldn't believe how bleak things looked. They now lacked even the most basic gear. They had no food. Rus felt as if he'd fallen down a staircase. Worst of all was Matt's weakening condition. The boy looked awful— pale, swollen, limp. He felt feverish. He talked in a disorganized mumble. How long could Matt stay alive if his health kept getting worse and worse?

Rus could scarcely restrain himself from hollering. He'd scream in frustration; he'd bellow in anger and fear. Not a good move, though, he told himself. Whatever else, he felt intent on avoiding anyone and everyone in the forest. Didn't they have enough trouble already? The last thing he and Matt needed was to cross paths with a bunch of headhunters.

38

Jodie sat against the trunk of a kapok tree and wept. All morning she had struggled to find her brothers, yet by now she admitted to herself that they'd somehow lost track of each other. She had found a few footprints on the riverbank, but only here and there; then the prints vanished into the forest. Calling out to them didn't accomplish anything. She had no idea where Matt and Rus were.

Terrible thoughts attacked her. Had they been dragged off by a jaguar? Chased by wild pigs? Or had they simply gone astray and, lacking even water now, wandered helplessly through the forest? She couldn't decide which of these calamities alarmed her most.

She stumbled down to the river. Kneeling in the mud, she cupped her hands, scooped water, and drank. The sun's reflection on the river dazzled her. She couldn't believe how weak she felt; it took all her strength to stand up again.

"Matt?" she said, scarcely raising her voice. "Rus?" Jodie flinched from the pain of missing them. Not just Matt—Rus, too. Both of her brothers.

Would she ever see them again? How would she find them in such a huge, complicated place?

Turning her back on the river, Jodie gazed at the forest. A wall of green. A tangle of foliage. Rising far above everything else was the kapok tree she'd been resting against. It must have been at least a hundred twenty feet tall, maybe taller. Nothing in the area rose anywhere as high as this enormous tree. With its massive buttressed trunk and all the thick vines spiraling around it, the kapok rose, a castle towering over the mere village surrounding it.

What sort of view, Jodie wondered, could she gain from such a height? Could she spot her brothers? Would her voice carry farther?

At once she staggered over to the tree and began to climb.

If she were climbing the tree itself, Jodie realized, she wouldn't have made it two feet off the ground. The trunk rose nearly straight up. Even the great wall-like buttresses angling off the trunk were almost vertical. Moss covered the bark, soft as dark green velvet. Plants grew all over the tree, too: tiny ferns; a fringe of little shoots; disheveled bushy things; and, here and there, big tufts that resembled the tops of pineapples. No, she wouldn't have gotten far on the tree alone. But it wasn't just the tree that Jodie climbed. Just as the kapok tree served as a kind of planter for all sorts of leafy vegetation, it also provided a structure to support the vines. *Lianas*: Jodie recalled the name from a book she'd read. Big vines that dangled from the kapok's branches. Some were small, just an inch or a half-inch thick. Others were big—two or three inches in diameter. And these vines were what made her climb possible.

A cluster of dark, tough vines dangled right next to the trunk. Taking hold of one in both hands, Jodie held tight, then placed her right foot on the trunk about two feet off the ground. She boosted herself up. Her right leg supported her, and her hands on the vine kept her in place. Then her left foot gave another boost. Then the right. The left again. Glancing down, Jodie saw she'd already made it five feet off the ground.

It was easier than climbing the rope back home. The Coopers had a big oak tree in their back yard, and some years ago Dad had tied a one-inch rope onto a branch overhanging the lawn. Jodie had often climbed the rope, sliding her way upward just as she'd learned in gym class. She prided herself on being able to reach the branch overhead without pausing. The catch was that Rus

147

taunted her for this ability. *Tomboy!* he'd holler from below. *I thought girls were supposed to be feminine!*

The thought of Rus nearly made Jodie lose her grip. Struggling to hold onto the vine, Jodie looked down again. She had already climbed another five or six feet.

Jodie, fifteen feet up now, reached a place that was thick with foliage. Curved, sword-like leaves poked her in the face and obstructed her hands. She couldn't even see what to grab. Groping, she took hold of what she thought was a vine, pulled off a loose curl of bark, lost her balance, and nearly toppled backward off the tree. Only by grabbing hard with her right hand could she keep from falling. Panting hard, Jodie then got a more secure grip and continued upward.

Despite the leaves entangling and distracting her, though, something else made a difference: more vines. Vines not only dangled from the tree but also wound repeatedly around the trunk. Some were as thick as the cable-like vine in her hands, and their spirals around the tree created footholds that helped Jodie stay in place. Tugging herself upward, she worked her way higher with growing confidence.

Then she faltered. A rushing noise filled her head. She saw everything around her as if through lace curtains. She nearly passed out. "I can't," she said out loud. Back home, Jodie could always have escaped by sliding down the rope, but that method wouldn't work here. She had to keep a grip. But how? Her hands felt greasy with perspiration. Sweat dripped off her eyebrows into her eyes. Glancing downward, she couldn't believe how far away the ground looked. Thirty-five, forty, fifty feet...

A tiny gold and purple butterfly zipped by, turned, and alighted on a leaf only inches from Jodie's face. The insect clung there flexing its wings.

For a moment, Jodie felt dizzy with delight. "Well—*hi!*" she said abruptly.

The butterfly hopped into the air and zigzagged away.

Jodie, her spirits sinking, realized that nothing had changed. There was no easy way out. She had no alternative but to continue.

And so she did. Though her muscles ached, her lungs struggled, and her heart pounded, she forced herself upward. The lianas grew narrower but offered her enough bulk to keep her secure on the tree. Her feet found footholds on the vines spiraling up the trunk. Thirst and hunger raged within her, but she kept going.

Rus and Matt. . . Where were they now? Were they hurt? Lost? She had to do what she could for them. She had no choice. They had lost everything that could help them survive. All they had left was each other.

"Rus?" she called out weakly. "Matt?"

Glancing down, Jodie felt terrified to see how high she'd climbed. The trees that had risen around her now rose *toward* her. She could stare down into the cone of a palm tree's leafy branches. She could gaze onto the top of a tree with bushy, star-like leaves. Birds roosted far below her. Jodie felt sick with fear at the sights all around.

"Rus!"

No response.

"Matt!"

No answer.

She didn't know why, but she kept climbing. Her muscles took over even as her mind started to quit. She just kept climbing.

Somehow, Jodie told herself, she needed to reach the top. If she could see the view, things would be good again. Something up there would show her what to do.

Once again she caught sight of that little gold-and-purple butterfly. "You!" she whispered. It flapped away, rising effortlessly. Going up looked so easy!

Jodie pulled herself a few feet higher. Then a few feet more. She realized only then that, having followed one fork of the tree where its trunk divided, she had reached a point only ten or fifteen feet from the top of the highest branch.

Turning her head carefully, she found herself above everything else in sight. All the other trees lay below her. The forest rolled away, green surf, in every direction. Birds circled far above this dark, leafy ocean.

The world stretched away clear to the horizon. Stunned by its size and by the radiance of the morning light on the forest's endless green, Jodie stared in alarm and delight. She felt helpless yet somehow more powerful than she'd ever felt before.

Then, turning slightly toward where the sun angled up into the sky, she noticed something.

Smoke.

A narrow cone of smoke rose from the forest and spread into the air.

There are some things you can invent, Jodie told herself, and some things you can't.

You can't invent other people. You can't invent the help you need from other people.

She knew at once what she must do.

39

Shouldn't we stay put?" Matt asked as Rus led him through the forest. He couldn't keep up with his brother as they pushed their way through all the leaves and branches. "Isn't that what you're supposed to do when you're lost?"

"—too risky—"

"Rus, wait up!"

Turning only once to look back, Rus gestured for Matt to hurry.

Matt slowed and stopped. His head was splitting and his lungs felt ready to explode. "Rus—"

When Rus doubled back he said, "Look, the sooner we find Jodie—"

"I can't do this." Matt's legs started to melt. He dropped to his knees. The ground tilted once, twice, three times. Matt clutched at some plants for support as the forest began to spin around him. Shoving his head against some leaves, he waited for the trees to stop orbiting him.

Then he felt something on his back. Rus's arm. A voice said, "Keep going."

"I can't," Matt said.

"Just try." Was that Rus speaking? It must've been Rus.

"I don't feel good."

"I'll help you," Rus said, reaching out to him, "but we have to keep going."

Matt stared at Rus's hand. How could he do what his brother asked? Standing up seemed as difficult as flapping his arms like a bird and soaring away.

Rus didn't want to carry Matt, but he saw no alternative. The kid could barely stay upright. If Rus

151

didn't carry him, Matt would probably collapse. Then Rus would have to choose between staying put or abandoning his brother. Both choices were unacceptable. There was no way to avoid hoisting Matt up, lugging him piggyback, and stumbling through the forest.

Where was Jodie? Rus couldn't figure out what had happened to her. She had headed downstream the day before; she'd surely head upstream now. Yet he couldn't spot her anywhere.

"There she is!" Matt shouted.

"Where?"

"There!"

Rus turned but didn't see anyone. Trees, vines, bushes—but no people. "Must've been something else," he told Matt. "Maybe a bird."

"I *saw* someone," Matt mumbled.

"I don't think so."

"Maybe it was Mom."

Rus felt a tingle of alarm. "Matt, you're imagining things."

"Mom!"

"Shh!"

"Where's Jodie?"

"Don't worry, we'll find her."

They lumbered off, convinced they'd locate their sister but finding only more empty passageways in the maze surrounding them.

40

Jodie pushed through the forest. The task of climbing down the kapok tree had used almost all of her remaining energy; now she could barely walk. Grabbing at vines or branches helped. She picked up a big stick, too, and used it as a cane. Yet even with this assistance, she felt so unstable that she staggered and swayed.

The biggest problem was not knowing where to go. Foliage surrounded her like fog; nothing helped her find her way. Up in the tree, she had spotted the smoke slightly to the left of the rising sun, so she figured she'd keep the sun as her reference point. But that method didn't always work. The trees blocked her view of the sun, and wandering either to the right or the left threw her off course. She proceeded anyway. She couldn't think of anything else to do.

Jodie shoved her way through. Leaves thrashed against her face and branches jabbed at her, but she shielded herself and elbowed ahead. Whenever she stumbled, she rested briefly, then scrambled up again and went ahead.

She was resolute. She didn't care what obstacles she faced; she'd get past them. The thorn-barked trees scratching her, the vines entangling her, the fallen limbs blocking her, the roots tripping her—everything made her even more determined to proceed. She would keep going.

Only by locating some people could she survive.

Which people, though? A village? A mission? A scientific outpost?

She had no idea. Jodie felt sure only that crossing paths with other human beings would save her life. And maybe Matt's and Rus's, too.

41

Matt couldn't believe how thirsty he felt. Hungry, too, but thirsty beyond anything he'd ever imagined. Thirstier than when he'd had the flu and couldn't keep anything down. . . *"Mom?"* he called out.

"She's not here."

He forced his eyes open and found himself lying on the ground. A boy's face stared at him. Blue eyes. . . Messy blond hair. . . Skin full of bruises, welts, and sores. . . "Who are *you?*" Matt asked.

"Rus."

Oh yeah, Rus. His brother Rus. Matt felt less confused now and far less worried, but the painful thirst still burned deep within him.

"What's the matter?" Rus asked.

"I need water."

"The river's down there a ways."

"I can't. . ." Matt couldn't remember how to get up.

For a while he waited, dozing. He awoke with a start.

Where was Rus?

Suddenly water touched his lips. Matt struggled to drink. He gulped fast. The cup, though—it was *soft.*

Matt opened his eyes and saw what had happened: Rus had brought him water cupped in his own hands.

Trekking back and forth between the river and their resting place, Rus gave Matt as much water as possible, then guzzled some himself. They'd lie low all day and set out at night. That way, Rus and Matt could limit the risk of bumping into Indians; they'd proceed more safely.

But where to? Rus still didn't know. He couldn't see how they could hold up much longer. Matt wasn't even able to stay awake more than five or ten minutes at a time, much less keep moving. His skin felt hot to the touch; he didn't understand even the simplest questions. Rus could carry him short distances, but by now he felt too tired to withstand his brother's weight any longer. Lacking even his meager meals of raw fish, Rus felt almost too weak to make a fist. Faltering, Rus settled Matt against a mossy log and collapsed.

"Matt," he whispered.

"Hm?"

"Matt, listen to me."

The boy nodded vaguely.

"We're going to settle in," Rus said. "We'll settle in for the night."

"Hm?"

"We're safe here. We'll make camp." *Right,* Rus told himself. They had no tent, no gear, not even a water bottle. *Making camp* was just a pretty name for giving up.

"Hng," Matt said.

"What's that?" Rus could scarcely hear him.

"Hngr."

"What?" Then at once Rus understood. Matt had said he was hungry.

But there was a problem: Rus had no food.

Worse yet, he had *almost* no food.

Only the candy bar. The Milky Way—his last candy bar.

The one he'd saved to guarantee his own survival.

42

How long, Jodie asked herself, had she been struggling through the forest? Two hours, maybe three? Longer? Four, five, six? That didn't seem possible, yet she couldn't be sure one way or the other; she had no watch, she couldn't always see the sun overhead, and the effort itself went on and on. All she knew was that tangles of foliage faced her at every turn. Jodie pushed her way through without knowing if she was getting closer to her destination.

Now and then she stopped to rest. She sat on the forest floor. If ants crawled up her legs or mosquitoes alighted on her skin, she didn't even swat them. Catching her breath was hard enough.

Was it possible, she wondered, that all this effort would get them nowhere? Was it possible that everything they'd done would amount to nothing? The struggle to get organized. The work to improvise equipment. The raft. The fishing gear. The sun canopy. The effort to climb the kapok tree. Now this exhausting hike. Was it possible that the constant effort that she'd made to get along with Rus would be pointless, too? Possible that they'd gone to so much trouble but would ultimately gain nothing in return? Possible that they'd struggle all this time and still end up dying?

The thought terrified her. With sweat streaming down her face, Jodie felt more and more convinced that they'd lose their battle. They'd wander another day or two—separately now—and collapse. They'd die of thirst and fatigue. They'd never leave Peru, never reach home, never see Mom and Dad again.

She suddenly broke down and started sobbing. The scariest thing was to be here all alone. It would be bad enough to die, but to die with no one else nearby. . . .

Something caught her attention. Not something she saw or heard—something she smelled.

Smoke.

Campfire smoke.

Staggering through the forest, Jodie followed that odor as if were the breath of life. At times she worried that Rus might be right after all—maybe the Indians would be angry at outsiders—but she went ahead anyway. Her own memories drew her forth. A bonfire at summer camp. The wood stove at a mountain house in Utah. Even the fireplace back home in New Jersey. Anything as good-smelling as wood smoke couldn't be bad.

Suddenly she arrived. She stepped through a tangle of lean shrubs and found herself in a clearing.

Beyond rose a cluster of what must have been houses. No walls, just corner posts. Long thatched roofs—grass or palm leaves.

She saw someone at a distance but couldn't decide if it was a man or a woman.

A rooster crowed: *Err-a-err-a-ERR!*

And people started coming out to see her.

157

43

W hat's this?" Matt asked in bewilderment. Some kind of warmth spread from his tongue to his mouth and down his throat. The feeling was so intense that his fingers tingled and flecks of light flashed before his eyes.

"Just eat," Rus said.

Matt couldn't help himself. His body felt ready to explode with delight. "What *is* it?"

"Milky Way."

"But where'd you get it?"

"Picked it off a tree," Rus said. "They grow on trees here in the rainforest."

Grow on trees? Matt felt confused; he couldn't understand the words. He just chewed on the candy his brother held out, and a deep sense of calm and reassurance spread through his body.

Now what? Rus asked himself.

While Matt lay motionless on the ground, Rus tried to figure out his next move. As if—he told himself—there was any move left to make.

They'd never get out of the rainforest alive; that much he knew. But Rus wasn't about to capitulate without a struggle. He'd take their little corner of the forest and make it a fortress. Moving as quickly as exhaustion allowed, Rus gathered branches and heaped them around the old log where Matt lay resting. He tore fronts off the palm trees and piled them on the branches. Then he crawled inside the castle he'd created, hunkered down, and waited.

He'd tried to protect Mom, Rus told himself, but he'd failed. Failed to convince her not to drink. Failed to help her hold down a job. Failed to protect her health.

Failed, in her last days, to keep her alive. He would have done anything for his mother, and he'd tried, but he'd failed.

Rus decided right then that he wouldn't let this happen again to someone he cared about.

With a heavy stick ready in his hands, Rus sat there gazing out through the leaves.

He'd do whatever he could to protect Matt, or else die trying.

44

The Indians didn't look the way Jodie had expected. No grass skirts. No feather headdresses. No body paint. No sticks in their cheeks or wooden plugs in their lower lips. Some of the youngest children were naked, but the adults wore familiar clothes—T-shirts and jeans or shorts for the men, baggy blouses and skirts for the women. Most of the men were bare-chested. Both the men and the women had long black hair and reddish-brown skin. Many of them went barefoot, though a couple of the men wore knee-high black rubber boots. Approaching, they spread out and formed a circle that surrounded her.

Her knees shook so hard that Jodie almost couldn't stay upright. Would they hurt her? Would they chop her up, as Rus had predicted? Alarmed, she glanced about. Two men carried huge, long-bladed knives. Another held a double-barreled gun. The sight of those weapons terrified her. No one aimed anything at her, though, and she saw no spears, war clubs, or blowguns.

Jodie raised her hands, palms out, to show they were empty and harmless. *"Hola,"* she said, barely able to talk. *"Buenos días."*

She waited, trembling, for someone to strike her.

All they did was stare.

They spoke among themselves, fast and low, in words that sounded like people talking in their sleep.

"I need help," she blurted, now in English. "Please help me." Jodie motioned desperately toward the forest at her back. "My brothers—"

The sight of these people grew faint. Jodie stumbled, trying to stay on her feet. Then a hissing noise filled her ears, and the ground came rushing up at her.

45

Someone shook him.

Was he late for school? No, Matt told himself, it was too hot for the school year. Summer camp, then. He was late for summer camp.

Matt—wake up!

Matt struggled to avoid the voice nagging him. Then he forced himself to turn.

"Rus?"

"Someone's coming!" Rus whispered.

"Huh?" Matt felt awful. He could barely force his eyes open.

"Shh! I think it's the Indians!"

Rus crouched among the bushes and tried to spot his pursuers. He couldn't see them, but he heard people pushing through the foliage and talking in low voices. How many? He couldn't tell. Lots more than he'd feared even in his worst nightmares—ten, fifteen, maybe more. Right, left, and straight ahead. Indians all over the place. A raiding party. Practically a whole tribe.

"Rus—"

He clapped a hand over Matt's mouth. The kid was half out of his head—too weak to help but too confused to follow orders. Feverish, Matt would call out and give away their hiding place, yet restraining him made Matt struggle even harder.

Then, peering through the leaves, Rus caught sight of the Indians. Just what he dreaded most: bare-chested men with lots of weapons. Not bows and arrows but shotguns and gigantic knives. Big blades they'd use to hack him to pieces. . .

Rus couldn't imagine how they'd escape. Matt could scarcely move. Rus himself felt weak from hunger,

161

thirst, and fatigue. He saw five or six Indians—no, eight or ten—passing just a dozen feet away.

Grabbing the stick he'd found, Rus realized that he *wouldn't* escape. He'd never succeed in fighting off these guys.

Still, he wouldn't give up. He'd go down fighting. He'd do anything possible to defend himself and Matt against these attackers.

Someone hollered.

Voices shouted back.

Suddenly the forest seemed full of people, people calling out, many of them right beside the bushes where Rus crouched over Matt.

They were surrounded.

Rus sprang up, raising his stick like a sword.

46

Rus!"

Jodie couldn't believe it, but Rus was alive. The Indians had found him, alive, in the forest. She pushed past the men and rushed over.

He nearly brought a big branch down on her.

"Don't hit me!" she hollered. "It's me, Jodie!"

Rus looked so—confused. "What's going on?" he asked, lowering the branch.

"These people are helping us."

"Helping us!"

"They've rescued us." She couldn't believe how terrible he looked—dirty, dazed, muddy, bruised, and smudged with dry blood.

A weak cry came from the bushes near Rus.

Jodie recognized Matt's voice at once and eased through the branches to find her little brother. "Are you okay?" she asked. "Matt, it's me." He looked all wadded up and trembly, like a dog that's been hit by a car. Gazing up, he didn't seem to recognize her.

Some of the men helped to pick up Matt, and they carried him away.

Sky overhead, then branches, then sky again, then more branches, shady green and bright blue shifting one into the other and back again. Matt looked when he could and closed his eyes when the light dazzled him. Sometimes a piece of cloth hovered above his face, with small brown hands suspending the corners. Sometimes many hands lifted him, shifted him from one side to the other, gave him water to drink, placed food in his mouth.

Where was he?

In a cradle, Matt decided, for he rocked gently to and fro. Somewhere safe. Somewhere full of people looking after him.

He slept.

Rus had felt concerned about going with the Indians, but he was too exhausted to resist. Besides, everything that followed the Indians' arrival had reassured him. The men who'd found him and Matt had treated them well. People at the village had given him food and water. Men, women, and children had come to stare but didn't hurt them. Rus, Jodie, and Matt had been allowed to sleep most of that afternoon and all night.

Should he have struggled or run away? Rus felt so weak that he wanted only to cooperate. And of course he felt deeply, bewilderingly pleased to eat the food these people brought: some kind of creamy fruit that tasted like pineapple, chunks of roasted meat, and a dense, waxy substance resembling boiled potato. Eating eagerly, Rus took whatever these people gave him.

Yet he kept expecting the sudden sweetness of this situation to turn sour. There would be harsh words in a language Rus didn't understand. Someone would start shoving him around. The illusion of safety would quickly turn to danger. Rus couldn't shake the fear that he'd end up simmering chest-deep in a pot of broth while the Indians, whooping and hollering, danced all around. But that didn't happen. He spent most of that first day dozing in a hammock. The women—one old, one young—waited nearby. A naked boy about three years old played in the dirt with a puppy. Some bare-chested men sat in the shade and spoke in murmury voices. When the afternoon rainstorm hit, ten or twelve people sat near Rus, all of them under the same thatched roof, until the shower ended. That was it. The only events occurred when someone came over to check on Rus, Jodie, and Matt.

Rus couldn't figure it out. These people seemed to be taking care of him.

Him—Rus Cooper.

Maybe Jodie was right after all.

That had been yesterday. In the morning, after they'd rested, a whole group had trekked through the forest to a river, then set out in seven or eight big gray wooden canoes, each ten or twelve feet long, that rode low in the water. Rus, Jodie, and Matt each boarded a separate boat. Five or six Indians climbed into each one, too. Not only men, but women and children as well— half the village, it seemed—had set off together. Bringing baskets and cloth bundles, they came along, several dozen of them, as if nothing mattered more than dropping their daily tasks and going downstream with three battered, sunburned, bug-bitten gringos. A festive air accompanied the travelers.

Rus half-sat, half-lay in the canoe and stared at the forest. Trees, vines, bushes, and flowers came and went. Birds alighted on nearby limbs and sprang off again as the flotilla passed. The canoes traveled faster than the raft had, though not by much—the Indians paddled slowly, as though saving strength for a long haul.

When he turned to Jodie, he found her slouched, asleep, in the canoe next to the one he rode. He couldn't believe how terrible she looked. Blood and dirt matted her hair; sunburn blistered her skin; scratches, cuts, and bruises left her face misshapen. The sight of her left Rus feeling faint—torn between the urge to help his sister and the realization of how little he could do. He wanted to protect her and felt shaken to know that he couldn't.

Matt lay motionless in another boat, where two women looked after him and the two babies they'd brought along. Matt—his brother. How was it possible, Rus wondered, that he'd allowed Matt to suffer so much? Couldn't he have done more? Protected him better?

Found him more food? Yet what could he have done, really, given the problems they'd faced? Rus didn't know. All he knew was that while staring at Matt where he lay in the boat, Rus worried about him, feared that such a small boy wouldn't survive all the damage he'd suffered, and hoped with all his might that they'd somehow reach safety in time.

Rus glanced around. People looked back at him without hostility. A tall young man whose hair resembled a black bowl capping his head. A woman with a sleeping baby slung in a cloth on her back. Three teenage boys and some middle-age men who paddled the boats with leaf-shaped oars. A ten- or twelve-year-old girl whose pet—a black puppy-faced monkey the size of a squirrel—rode on her shoulder. An old man whose grinning mouth contained only a single tooth.

Why, Rus asked himself, should he agree to accompany these people? He didn't know. He wasn't sure what they'd do with him. It was all a big gamble. Yet somehow, in ways he'd never felt before, Rus felt both the need and the desire to stop resisting and let them take care of him.

Do you espeak Espanish?" the man asked Jodie as he helped her from the canoe onto the riverbank. What she noticed about him first was that he wore a Boston Red Sox baseball cap. He had some gold front teeth. And he gazed at her with the warmest eyes she could imagine.

She shook her head and suddenly felt overwhelmed. They had reached a town—a much bigger place than the Indian village they'd left behind—and she understood now that she was safe. An odd moment for falling apart, she decided, but she couldn't help it. Clutching the man, she sobbed in his arms.

The man patted her on the shoulder. "I espeak a little bit the English," he said. "We will communicate ourselves very well."

This man, along with other people at the dock, helped Jodie and Rus climb a wooden staircase built into the riverbank. More steps than she expected: twenty, thirty. . . ? Jodie could scarcely walk. Worried about falling, she went ahead only because people on both sides supported her. Where was Rus? She saw him right ahead. "Where's Matt?" she asked abruptly. "My little brother?"

"People help him," said a voice.

"We take good care of you," said another.

After what seemed a nearly endless climb up the wooden staircase, Jodie found herself at the top of a mud cliff. The river below looked much bigger than any she'd seen since leaving Iquitos—far narrower than the Amazon but two or three times wider than the little tributary she had rafted down. Green from all the trees' reflection, the water extended right and left for hundreds of yards. Canoes moved silently along both shores. On the opposite bank, a group of women washed laundry in the river, and nearby some children splashed about loudly.   The scene facing Jodie seemed ordinary yet almost magical.   That there could be so many people! That she could be among them, safe!

What she saw when she turned, however, startled her even more.

A soccer game.

Jodie walked away from the staircase she'd climbed and found herself on a huge, flat field. Thatched wooden houses rose at the field's edges.   In the space between the houses, two teams of young men battled over a ball zigzagging among them.   Surrounding the field stood spectators, mostly teenagers. All of these people were black-haired and copper-skinned. Some wore sports outfits—soccer jerseys, shorts, knee-high socks, and athletic shoes.   Most of the spectators wore T-shirts, shorts, and sandals or tennis shoes. Having expected to find more traditional attire among the people here—hand-decorated homespun clothes, perhaps—Jodie stared at this gathering in bewilderment.

"Goal!" someone yelled.

The crowd cheered.

Rus turned to Jodie and raised one eyebrow. "Can you believe it?"

Then, not suddenly but steadily, flowing like a river, people started to come over. A man spoke to her in Spanish, and someone else began to translate.

"My name is Jodie," she stammered, "and our plane crashed."

Part Five

The Airport

TRUST

he wrote in the condensation on the glass.

Six days later, while waiting for the flight from Iquitos to Miami, Rus stared out through the window at the airport waiting lounge. The rainforest rose just a few hundred feet beyond the tarmac. Palm trees. Great trees tangled with vines. A green wall of saplings and bushes. The rainforest.

He couldn't believe they'd somehow made it out of there alive. The place would loom forever in his memory. The infinite foliage. The river. The sun and rain. The thirst, hunger, and exhaustion. Scratching his bug bites, Rus could still hear the mosquitoes' whine and feel the tropical heat even though he stood in the airport's air conditioned comfort. He felt amazed to be there.

How was it possible that they'd survived? So much had gone wrong. The plane crash. The limited equipment. The lack of food. The loss of the raft. The false steps they'd taken. The mistakes they'd made. The bad luck they'd suffered. For a long time, everything had deteriorated hopelessly.

He rubbed out the initial T.

RUST

Somehow he'd held steady. He'd stayed confident of his own strengths and abilities, and he'd done whatever had been necessary to get by.

Was it wrong, he wondered abruptly, to have relied so much on himself? Surely no one could hold that

171

against him. Didn't you have a right to save your own skin? A responsibility, even?

He rubbed out the other T.

RUS

But Rus could see now that simply looking after himself wasn't what had saved him. He focused his eyes differently and saw the reflection in the window: not the forest beyond, not his own image in the glass, but the people behind him in the waiting lounge. Jack, seated in a plastic chair. Matt, curled up against his father. Jodie, slouched against Jack on his other side. He felt a twinge of unfamiliar delight when he looked at them. It didn't make sense, but somehow he'd saved his own skin by looking after these other people. And they'd saved their skins by looking after him.

Jodie must have caught sight of Rus staring at her, for she got up just then and walked over. "How's it going?" she asked.

"Okay," he answered.

She noticed his name on the glass. "What's this?"

"Nothing."

"You're autographing the airport?"

"It's a game I play."

"The plane'll be here soon," she said.

He nodded. He couldn't wait to be back. Back with his family.

With his right index finger, Rus stroked the R on the window.

US

"What's it mean?" Jodie asked.

He nudged her gently in the ribs. "You figure it out."